The
Jungle

The
Jungle

✮ ✮ ✮

Pooja Puri

INK ROAD

First published 2017 by Ink Road

INK ROAD is an imprint and trade mark
of Black and White Publishing Ltd.

Black & White Publishing Ltd
29 Ocean Drive, Edinburgh EH6 6JL

1 3 5 7 9 10 8 6 4 2   17 18 19 20

ISBN: 978 1 78530 088 2

A CIP catalogue record for this book is available from the British
Library.

Supported by
The National Lottery®
through Creative Scotland

Typeset by Iolaire, Newtonmore
Printed and bound by Nørhaven, Denmark

Author's Note

Much of the action of this story takes place in Calais, France. Here, on the border between land and sea, formerly lay the migrant encampment more commonly known as "the Jungle". Its inhabitants came from far and wide – some to find a better life for themselves, others to escape political violence and war. The difficulties they endured on their journeys are unimaginable. Life in "the Jungle" was not much better. Facilities were, at best, basic; at worst, non-existent. There was little food. Charities did what they could but resources were limited.

While writing this book, I have tried to present as accurate a picture of the camp as I can. However, it is important to note that this story and its characters are a work of fiction. As such, there may be inevitable distortions between "the Jungle" as it existed in real life and the setting presented in the book. I hope, nonetheless, that in reading about Mico and Leila, readers can start to understand the despair and courage of those willing to risk everything for a brighter future.

1

Mico was stealing.

He was lying in the dusty undergrowth, hidden by a screen of dense shrubbery. A thin layer of sweat had collected beneath his clothes; tufts of dirt and leaves clung to him like a second skin.

He inched forward. Ahead of him stood the tent. There were hundreds like it here, rising up from the ground like giant anthills. Small dots of people milled about them, their voices carrying across the air in an endless watery babble. If Mico closed his eyes he could almost imagine he was back home, fishing for squeakers or redfins. Almost.

The tent had been propped open with a bucket for ventilation, leaving just enough of a gap for him to see inside. In contrast to its neighbours, it was kitted out with everything: pans, clothes, a radio, chairs – real wooden ones, not the cobbled scraps used in the rest of the camp. The bread was on a table. Just looking at it made Mico's stomach hurt.

Slowly he raised himself onto his haunches. He had

been careful. He'd waited at the front of the camp until he'd seen the men leave. The newspapers called them people smugglers, but here they had a different name. They were the Ghost-Men. The men with magic; the spirits who could pass through borders without being seen.

There were always two of them. One was built like a crow, tall and beady-eyed; the second was a lizard, short with stumpy legs and stumpy arms. It was him you had to watch out for. Almost unconsciously, Mico raised his hand to his left shoulder. The skin had almost healed but there was a scar there now, a gift from the Lizard's belt. He narrowed his eyes. One day, he hoped to return the favour.

Sometimes, the Ghost-Men would have other people with them, but today they had left alone. Mico had watched until they were no longer in sight of the camp entrance. He'd counted another five minutes just in case they'd forgotten anything. Then he'd crept the long way round the back of the tents. He'd made sure to stay deep in the bushes so that nobody would see him.

There were always plenty of people waiting for the Ghost-Men. Mostly new arrivals. They'd wash up on Calais hoping the Ghost-Men would help them. But the Ghost-Men were businessmen. Only if you could afford it would they spin their spell and help you disappear. Like him, most of them wanted to start a new life in England. For seven hundred pounds you'd get a place in a truck. It wasn't the most secure option. Not now there seemed to be police on nearly every single checkpoint. Better to go in a car boot. Officers didn't like stopping ordinary vehicles so as long as you had a decent-looking driver you'd be safe. But you needed money. A lot of it.

Mico shifted uneasily. He did not want to think what the Ghost-Men would do if they found him in their tent. But the bread was only a few paces away now. He gritted his teeth, readying himself to spring.

Suddenly, there was a movement to the far left of him. Mico dropped down like a shot. He saw the grasses rustle. Little by little, a foot emerged, followed by a hand, then the mud-stained face of a boy. He glanced warily around him, before taking a couple of steps forward. He stopped again, his ears pricked for any sound. Finally satisfied he was alone, he darted towards the tent.

A knife of frustration stabbed through Mico as the boy snatched up the bread. For a moment, he thought about confronting him. He could threaten to reveal him to the Ghost-Men. Force him to hand the bread over. But the boy was a lot bigger than him. A bruise the size of an orange gleamed on his chin. One thing was for certain. Mico wouldn't be able to make him do anything.

He watched as the boy lay down on one of the camp beds. What was he doing? He had the bread. Why didn't he leave? But the boy was clearly in no hurry. Snatches of tinny-sounding music swelled into the air as he turned on the radio.

"Get out, stupid," whispered Mico.

The boy's head snapped up. Mico instinctively flattened himself against the ground but it was not him the boy had heard. Through the long grass in front of him he saw the Ghost-Men entering the tent. The Lizard came first. The Crow, as always, followed behind.

3

Everything seemed to flicker into fast motion. The boy leapt up like he'd been stung. The Lizard drew forward, snake-tongue flicking in and out.

"What you doing, kid?" Mico heard him say. The boy's reply was inaudible but the fear on his face blazed like fire. The Lizard turned and said something to the Crow who turned up the volume on the radio. The boy's eyes widened. He edged back, holding his hands in the air. His lips shaped the same word over and over. *Sorry*—

The Lizard didn't wait to hear any more. He grabbed the boy's collar and dragged him outside. A wave of nausea washed over Mico as the Lizard threw the boy to the ground. He curled up into a ball, hands over his head. The Lizard raised his boot. Mico shut his eyes. The radio rose over them in a shrill clamour, drowning the boy's howls.

At last it was over.

"Next time, I chop off your hands," hissed the Lizard, hauling the boy to his feet. The bruise on his chin had split open and a fat line of blood dribbled down his skin.

"Make sure you tell your friends."

The boy nodded, whimpering softly. The Lizard shoved him in the back, watching as he limped away through the grass. He was about to turn back when something made him pause. His eyes thinned as he scanned the foliage before him. Mico held his breath. The Lizard's tongue flicked in-out, in-out, tasting the air. Any second now he would realise Mico was there—

"Ai, Yasi," shouted the Crow. "New lot's here. We need to take delivery."

4

The Lizard remained stock-still, his gaze trained on Mico's hiding place.

"Come on, Yasi. They waiting for us at port."

With a slow swivel of his head the Lizard turned back to the tent. The radio sang. Deep in the grass, Mico stared at the drops of blood left behind on the dirt. If he screwed up his eyes he could almost imagine they were the silken tail of a redfin.

2

In the beginning, Mico had dreamed. He had watched an orange sun bleed across a red earth. He'd heard the skittering of crickets as they whispered secrets in the wild bush. He had smelled the evening wood smoke as Ma prepared the fire for cooking; felt the sting of Uncle's hand when he answered him back.

And then the dreams had stopped.

It had happened slowly like night creeping into day. At first, everything had just blurred around the edges but then it had started to darken. As if a thief had stolen into his head and, bit by bit, taken his old life away. Now, when Mico tried to remember, he had to work extra hard. Every morning after waking up, he'd keep his eyes closed and squeeze his mind as tightly as he could, trying to picture everything he had left behind. Some days, it worked so well it was as if his entire town had exploded in his head. But those days were rare. Most of the time, it seemed, he could lie there for ever and remember hardly anything.

Today was one of those days.

Mico lay with his eyes closed for a minute longer, his mind searching out the face of his little sister, Esther. She'd been born with a large mole on the side of her face but he couldn't remember if it was on the left cheek or the right.

"Hey, Mico!"

Hassan's voice blasted like a foghorn above his face. Mico didn't move. He needed to remember.

"I know you're awake."

Mico felt a light kick against his leg.

"Come on. I need your help."

Mico turned back into his blanket. Already, Esther's face had started to swim out of focus.

"Get lost, Hassan."

There was a loud sigh.

"Then I guess I'll have to eat this without you."

At once, Mico's eyes flew open. Remembering was always harder on an empty stomach.

"Cheese sandwiches," said Hassan, triumphantly holding up a paper bag.

Mico's eyes widened. There was a charity-run kitchen in the camp which was supposed to give them one meal a day, but priority was given to the women and kids. If you left early enough you might get a handout but there was never enough food to go round. In any case, the kitchen wouldn't open until later.

"Where'd you get those?"

"Move over and I'll tell you."

Mico sat up and shifted himself sideways so that there was enough space on the floor for both of them. Hassan removed a handkerchief from his pocket and dusted his seat before sitting down.

7

"There's one for each of us," he said, handing Mico a sandwich. "You, me and Sy. Where is he?"

Mico shrugged as he wolfed down the food. Sy, or Syed, was the third tent member. Most of the time he was outside the camp doing odd jobs for the locals. Even when he was in he preferred not to talk much. "A silent horse", Mico's Ma would have called him.

"I'll keep his for later," said Hassan, wrapping Sy's breakfast into his handkerchief. Mico forced himself to keep a straight face.

"Did you nick them?" he asked, as Hassan pulled a third sandwich out the bag.

Hassan snorted.

"You think I'm Razi now?"

"Razi's smart," said Mico loyally.

Hassan flattened the paper bag onto his lap and placed the sandwich on top of it.

"Razi is an arrogant weasel," he said brusquely. "Strutting about like he owns the place."

Mico bit back a smile. Razi was only a couple of years older than him, seventeen at most, but he behaved like a fully grown man. He was as thin as a stick with long, stringy arms and a quick, clever face. Mico had first encountered him a few weeks after his arrival. Back then, he'd been sharing a tent with another family. They'd had a spate of rough weather and the tarpaulin had been lashed so bad one side had almost ripped off. Mico had just finished securing the last corner in place when he'd become aware of the older boy watching him.

"Not bad," the stranger had said, eyeing the tent approvingly. "You got good hands. You want real work?"

8

He spoke quickly, his words loose marbles, rolling and bumping into each other. Mico had shrugged, taken aback by the boy's confidence. It sparkled off him like raindrops, shiny and reckless.

"I got bikes need fixing. No money, but I get you something. Come, come."

Before Mico could reply he'd already started giving directions to his tent.

"Mine is third line that way. Second to end."

At Mico's blank stare, he'd grinned.

"Razi," he said, slapping his chest. "Ask for the name. Someone send you."

And that was how it had started. For months now, Razi had been smuggling bikes into the camp, stealing them off the locals and selling them on. If they were damaged he'd call on Mico to see if he could fix them. It wasn't a fair partnership. Razi pocketed all the money from the sales, but as promised he always made sure Mico got something. Food mostly – crisps, chocolate, sometimes gum. It helped, of course it did, but it was never enough. Mico was always hungry.

"You should stay away from him," said Hassan. "He'll get in trouble one of these days and take you with him."

As he spoke, he rolled up his sleeves and, after a lengthy inspection of his hands, started to eat. Mico watched in faint amusement. Some people, when they ate, tore at their food. They didn't taste it really. It was more a question of speed.

His Uncle Abu had been one such person. He'd eat his meals like a general waging a battle – all rattling and clattering for a couple of minutes then a great long silence, broken by the occasional burp.

Hassan, in comparison, ate like a bird. He would peck at his food as if it were a dangerous creature that at any moment might turn around and bite him. He was the complete opposite to Razi, thoughtful and handsome with a soft, gentle mouth that forever seemed to be frowning. Back home, he had taught English but what he really wanted was to become an actor.

"If you didn't steal them where they from?" asked Mico.

"There was a man giving food parcels at the front of the camp," said Hassan, nibbling a tiny corner of bread. He ate so slowly that it took all of Mico's willpower not to snatch the sandwich away for himself.

"An English man. Said he'd seen us on the news and wanted to help."

"Did he have a car?"

"I didn't ask."

"Why not? If he really wanted to help, he could drive us to England."

"It's not that easy, Mico."

"Why not?"

Hassan sighed with impatience.

"Why can't you just be grateful for the food and leave it at that? It's not every morning we get sandwiches."

"It's not every morning you see an English man who might have a car."

"I've told you before, Mico. I'm not going to be taken to England like a piece of luggage. Oh, you can make as many faces as you want. The first time I went on a truck the Ghost-Men took our money and loaded us in like fish in a crate. There were about twenty of us. All stuck in the dark, rolling into each other."

10

"Police don't check cars as much," Mico mumbled.

Hassan didn't seem to hear him.

"We didn't even get halfway before the police stopped us. One of the men got so frightened when he heard them banging on the door he had a heart attack."

Mico stared at him. Hassan had never told him this part of the story before.

"What happened to him?"

"I don't know. The police didn't want us hanging around. We were sent back before the ambulance arrived."

He swallowed the last of his sandwich and wiped his fingertips on the edge of his shirt.

"Mood's still tense out there," he murmured.

Mico looked down at his hands, his heart thudding in his chest. Guilt flooded through him as he thought of what he'd witnessed at the Ghost-Men's tent. The story had sped round the camp as quick as wildfire. Just thinking about it made Mico shrink a little inside. He hadn't done anything to help. He'd just hidden in the grass.

Next to him, Hassan continued talking but Mico was no longer listening. Deep down, he knew he'd probably done the right thing. His Ma had always said there was a fine line between being brave and acting reckless. Every night she would hook up a line of bells above the front door. These were supposed to frighten the *jinn*, the night spirits that crept into people's bedrooms and fed on their dreams and fears. Uncle Abu used to laugh. Superstitious nonsense, he said. Ma's reply was always the same. "Why should we take the chance?"

11

The Ghost-Men were no different to the *jinn*. Let them too close and they would swallow you whole. There were plenty of stories about them in the camp. They were criminals, murderers, bounty hunters. They were once mercenaries scavenging from one war to another. They had contacts to the highest level of French government. So many tales spinning around that it was almost impossible to tell the truth from the lies. But with every whispered rumour, the Ghost-Men grew a little more terrible, a little less human.

What the Lizard had done to that boy wasn't Mico's fault but he couldn't help feeling responsible somehow. He was ashamed too. Ashamed that he'd stayed in the grass, ashamed for hiding like a coward.

"You all right?"

Hassan was looking at him with concern.

Mico forced a smile.

"I was thinking about that kid."

He wondered what Hassan would think if he knew the whole truth. For a moment, he thought about telling him everything. Then he thought better of it. Hassan was a friend but sometimes he behaved more like his mother. Fussing and clucking as if Mico was still a baby that needed looking after. He'd never hear the end of it.

Hassan shrugged.

"He asked for it. Only an idiot would steal from the Ghost-Men."

"Can't blame him for trying," muttered Mico.

There was a sudden rustling outside the tent as Sy walked in. He was a tall man with the build of a wrestler. His face, like the rest of him, was big and square. His eyes were a deep brown and tough as desert sand. Every time he came into the tent, he seemed to bring a little darkness in with him; or perhaps, Mico thought, it was just that the shadows collected more readily around his form than anywhere else.

He nodded at them as he entered. His hands and cheeks were flecked with red paint.

"Where you been, Sy?" said Hassan.

Sy, as usual, responded with a grunt.

"I got you a sandwich."

Sy grunted again and rubbed himself roughly with a flannel. Then he took off his coat and lay down on top of it. Less than a minute later, he was snoring.

"I better get going," whispered Hassan. "I promised Sara I'd keep an eye on Tamal for a while."

"Again?"

Sara and Hassan had come over on the same boat. They weren't related but Hassan made a point of looking out for her.

Hassan shrugged.

"It gives her a break. Besides, she's going to cook me dinner." He ruffled Mico's hair. "It's a good deal. I'll bring some back if I can."

Mico made a face.

"Not the slop you brought last time."

Hassan cuffed him round the ear and stood up. He had to hunch to stop his hair scraping the dust on the ceiling.

Mico knew that Hassan kept a small mirror in his shirt pocket. At night, when he thought nobody was watching, he would take it out and draw his hands across his face, pinching the skin between his fingers in swift, agitated movements. He looked so scared as he did it that once, or twice, Mico had very nearly called

13

out to him. But he knew he couldn't. This nightly ritual was Hassan's secret. In the camp, where they already owned so little, it seemed right to let him keep this one thing for himself.

"Don't eat Sy's sandwich," said Hassan as he clambered out of the tent.

Mico threw him a finger in reply.

3

Almost as soon as Hassan was gone a silence settled across the tent. It wasn't a perfect silence. It could never be that. The movement and chatter of the people outside pulsed through the air without end. It was the kind of noise that beat in colour and thrummed with warmth. Hassan was forever complaining about it but Mico didn't mind. The sounds reminded him of home.

They had lived on the edge of town; him, Esther, Ma, Uncle Abu and about a hundred chickens. Mico's father, Jac, had started the farm. He had died before Mico was born. Uncle Abu had handled the business ever since. Bit by bit he had saved enough to buy more land, more birds. Esther loved them. Sometimes, after school, she'd take a bucket of feed and walk through the pens, chattering and stroking their feathers.

Mico didn't know how she did it. He hated the chickens, hated their endless shrieking, their stinky feathery smell. Once, in a fit of temper, he had told his uncle they should farm horses instead. Uncle Abu had laughed.

"I said the same to your father when we started the business. Why chickens, I ask him. Chickens teach us about life, he says. Everything we need to know we can learn from a chicken."

"But they're noisy," Mico argued. "And they make all that mess."

Uncle Abu looked over at Esther and winked.

"Do you hear your brother?" he said. "He's talking like the baobab."

Esther had laughed.

There were many tales about the baobab. Some said that if you ate its fruit, a lion would eat you. Others said that if you drank from it, you would be protected against crocodile attacks. Esther's favourite was the one about the gods. In it, the baobab was one of the first trees to appear on the land. It should have been proud, but it was a jealous thing, always looking to its neighbour. So when the gods created the palm tree, the baobab whined that it wanted to be taller. When it saw the fig tree, it wanted its fruit. And when it saw the beautiful flame tree, it cried out for its blossoms. Eventually, the gods got so angry that they pulled the tree from its roots and stuck it back into the earth upside-down so that they wouldn't have to listen to its whining.

An ache grew in Mico's chest as he thought of his sister. He had looked for her every day when he had first arrived in the camp. He knew it was impossible, but still, deep down, he warmed the hope that she too might have got away. But every new shipment was followed by the same wave of hopelessness. Now he'd stopped trying. He could no longer bear the disappointment.

16

Sy coughed in his sleep and murmured something in a foreign language. Mico watched him for a few moments then turned away, embarrassed.

One day, as a treat, Uncle Abu had taken him to the city. There, he had visited his first museum. The place had fascinated and repelled him. There, history was told through bones. There, it was not the living that spoke, but the dead.

In a way they weren't much different to those fossils; Hassan, Sy, even Mico himself, each of them stranded on these shores like forgotten relics. Sy was from Afghanistan. Sometimes, at night, Mico would hear him whimpering but Sy never spoke about his nightmares afterwards. Whatever demons lurked in his past were his own. Hassan was from Syria. He had been forced to leave when war broke out. Mico had travelled from Kenya. Together, they were almost a whole continent.

They had divided the tent into three sections – Hassan in the middle, while Mico and Sy had a corner each. Hassan was the tidiest. He had a cushion, a small yellow bucket (which functioned as a stool and sink), a couple of T-shirts, a spare pair of trousers and some magazines with the faces of American film stars plastered across them.

Sy's corner was empty. Mostly because Sy kept everything of value in his coat, which had more pockets in it than seemed possible.

Mico's own corner was furnished solely with a blanket. It had been given to him by a charity worker and smelled entirely of dog. Or, when it rained, wet dog. Still, it kept him warm. Next to the blanket, he kept a jacket (another donation), a toothbrush (his own) and a pocketknife (his uncle's). With a surreptitious glance

17

at Sy, Mico slid his hand underneath the rough fabric of the blanket and pulled the knife out. Then he slipped it into his pocket and stood up.

The smell rose to meet him as soon as he stepped out the tent. He staggered backwards, momentarily overwhelmed. This was no ordinary stink. It came at you like a bully, vicious, demanding attention. He had lived with the stench for nearly a year now, but still the force of it surprised him. It was rubbish and sweat, old clothes and unwashed bodies all thrown into one.

The French authorities had installed a few portable showers at one end of the camp, but there was always a queue for them. They weren't regularly maintained either. Mico had tried them once. He hadn't bothered going again. What was the point? Even if he did wash himself, there was no getting away from the smell in the camp. It stuck to the air. It found its way into your blood. You were part of it, no matter how hard you scrubbed yourself.

Squaring his shoulders, Mico started away from the tent. One of the first things he had learnt when he arrived was that it was important to look tough. There were not many Africans here, and he was in the minority. The side of the camp where he lived was filled with young men eager to prove they were no longer boys. They were bored and angry – a dangerous combination at the best of times.

So Mico was careful. When he walked through the camp, he straightened his back and broadened his chest. He didn't make eye contact, but neither did he look at the ground. He had to look tough enough so that nobody would mess with him, but not so tough as

18

to be a threat. It was a tricky balance to get right, but after months of practice he was a master at it. And just in case, he had the knife.

Men stood outside their tents smoking (if they were lucky or clever enough to have cigarettes) or talking and watching others smoke. Some wheeled around on bikes, most of them bought or bartered from Razi. Many wore bandages. Sometimes, when business was bad, Razi organised bike races to raise some extra cash. Fights also occasionally broke out between different groups, but there was another, bigger reason for the injuries. Those who couldn't afford the Ghost-Men would often try jumping trains in the Tunnel. It was stupid and dangerous but if you made it you had yourself a one-way ticket to England. Free of charge.

The camp was spread across two open fields. Tents spilled across the land as far as the eye could see, tarpaulin sheets flapping open like gaping wounds. In several places, the grass had long surrendered to the trample of feet. Trails of mud formed deep, knobbly ridges across the ground. When it rained, pools of water would collect across the earth, transforming it into a sea of rust-coloured sludge. Then each tent became an island, a tiny floating world.

To new arrivals the camp looked like a maze, but beneath the confusion lay a system. There were three main areas – one for men, one for women and another for families. To begin with, people had dumped rubbish anywhere, but that had caused problems when rats started to run riot. Most of the trash was now discarded in the woods which bordered the rear of the camp. A road leading to the port snaked past on the opposite side.

In every direction, flags fluttered across the tops of tents, marking bits of land into individual colonies: Iraq, Sudan and others which Mico didn't recognise. Geography had never really interested him. His teacher, Mr Bancho, had been a toad of a man. Mico had often been sent out of class for talking or daydreaming, and had spent many a happy afternoon sitting outside, watching the odd lizard as it crawled across the white-washed walls.

Perhaps if he had bothered to work harder, the flags would have meant something to him. Perhaps he would have found out why they were so powerful.

He had not gone far when he spotted the Doctor. He was sitting cross-legged on the ground, rolling a toothpick into his ear. His feet were bare. As always, a pair of brown sandals were carefully laid out on a piece of newspaper beside him.

"Mico Baba," he said, waving him to stop. His voice was rough like sandpaper.

"Come, come. Sit, sit."

He patted the ground in front of him.

"How are you, Baba? Good, good, hm?"

Mico shrugged.

"Same as I was yesterday. Same as I'll be tomorrow."

The Doctor nodded seriously. He had a thin face with round glasses that were perched on a long, crooked nose. His skin was dark and wrinkled. A straggly beard hung down his chin like a moth-eaten curtain.

"All right, then. That's all right. Good, good, hm?"

Mico smiled in spite of himself. The Doctor was the oldest resident in the camp. He wasn't really a doctor but that was what everybody called him on account of his white coat. It was miles too big for him and still retained a strangely acidic smell from whichever institution had donated it. The Doctor never took it off.

"What are you doing out here?" asked Mico.

"I am waiting, yes. Ask me why."

"Why?"

"Because today is the day I leave from here. Good news, yes?"

Mico, who had heard this many times, said nothing.

"Ah, you are sad, yes," said the Doctor. "You think I won't remember you. The boy with hair that curls like wire. The boy with eyes that burn like fire. You see? It is like a song. Now you mustn't be sad, yes. I will not forget you, Mico." He tapped the side of his head with the toothpick. "I am old, yes, but there is life up here yet."

"When are you going?"

The Doctor raised his hand to his head and looked up at the sky.

"Not yet. But soon, yes." He beamed. "The governments, they have realised, yes. They know they cannot keep me here. I am an old man, not an animal."

"That's not what the newspapers say," Mico murmured. "Don't you know what they call this place?"

The Doctor wasn't listening.

"Yes, yes," he said, holding his sandals up in the air. "Soon, I can wear these. Not here, not yet."

He placed them back on the paper.

"Home," continued the Doctor, his face glowing. "There is a town in England, yes. Crawley. You must go. It is a wonderful place, yes. The people, very friendly. The football, not so good. I ran a shop there. I sold newspapers, yes, for nearly fifty years. Good, good, all good,

21

hm." The Doctor's eyes tightened suddenly. "This is what I tell them when they come to take me away. I say, I have sold newspapers here for fifty years, yes. I support Crawley Town FC. At Christmas, I put the shiny stuff, yes, the shiny stuff, in my shop windows. I am English. But they tell me you have no papers. You have no papers, you cannot stay. So they send me back. To Sudan, yes. But that country is no longer my home. It is too hot. Not enough rain. Only now they see their mistake. They will come to take me back to Crawley, yes."

"What if they don't?"

The Doctor's eyes widened in surprise. Behind the enormous frame of his spectacles he looked like an owl.

"What if – ah, Mico. You silly boy. They will come."

If anyone else had spoken to him like that Mico would never have let them get away with it. But he knew the Doctor didn't mean it unkindly. He was so old that everyone looked like a child to him.

"I will sell newspapers again, hm. But what about you? What will you do when you leave this place?"

Mico fiddled with the torn lace of his trainers.

"I don't know," he said truthfully. He wanted to go to college in England, but he hadn't decided what he'd study when he got there. If he got there.

"Ah, you young people." The Doctor clicked his tongue in disapproval. "It is always the same with you, yes. When I was a boy, we had no choices. Now you have too many. My father told me to work, work he said, and I did. You are spoilt, yes. You have too much."

"Did your father tell you to go to England?" asked Mico, curious.

The Doctor looked suddenly evasive.

"What does that matter?"

He jabbed the toothpick at Mico.

"When I was young, hm, we weren't allowed to ask questions of our elders. Now go." He waved his hand at Mico like he was an irritating fly. "I am old man and I am tired. Come later, yes."

Mico sighed and pulled himself to his feet. He would have liked to sit with the Doctor a while longer, but there was no point staying. Not now he'd annoyed him. With a final look behind him, he balled his fists into his pockets and walked off.

4

"You are early," said Razi. "I thought you come later."

Mico shrugged. One of Razi's crew had found him watching a card game earlier that afternoon. He'd been told to come for the evening but he'd made his way over as soon as it had finished.

"I can come after if you want."

"No, no. You here now. Come look."

Razi was crouched over a pair of bikes. He had a strip of cloth tied around his head and black grease marks all over his face. In the tent behind him a few boys were patching together a sheet of plastic.

"Someone trash it," said Razi, following Mico's gaze. "Crazy, huh?"

Mico nodded in agreement. It was unbelievable what some people threw away. He turned his attention to the bikes. BMXs. They looked expensive, but one was in pretty bad shape. The wheel spokes were bent and the chain had twisted in on itself.

"You find these in someone's rubbish?"

Razi grinned slyly.

"Maybe."

Mico prodded the mangled chain.

"What happened to this one?"

Razi spat before answering.

"Police. They got Shakeel."

He looked more annoyed than concerned.

"What will you do?"

"Lay low. Few days. No Shakeel, I find someone else."

"What about me?"

"You?"

Razi stared at him for a second. When he realised Mico was serious, he broke into a grin and clapped him on the back.

"How old you are? Fourteen?"

"Fifteen," said Mico, forcing himself to keep his voice steady. "Sixteen in a couple of months."

"You a kid."

"I can handle it."

Razi was still smirking.

"You handle, huh? What happen when French police up your arse?"

"I'll be fine."

"What if you caught? Who fix my bikes?" Razi spat and rubbed his nose. "No. You better working here."

Mico looked back down at the bikes, embarrassment churning through him. He couldn't bear for Razi to see how much his words had stung. After all these months he still thought of him as a child. Just like Hassan.

He pulled savagely at the bike chain, wincing as the metal cut into his finger. A thin line of blood oozed out.

"Careful," warned Razi, popping a stick of gum into his mouth. "Those hands precious. You look after."

He held a second strip of gum out to Mico. A peace offering.

Mico didn't take it. Razi shrugged and put it in his mouth.

"Waste not," he winked. "So? Can you fix it?"

"Maybe."

"Maybe yes or maybe no?"

Mico didn't answer. He was watching the boys in the tent. They were all older than him, every one of them tough-looking and hard – the kind of guys you'd want with you in a fight. No wonder Razi had laughed at his suggestion. He had nothing on them, except perhaps—

"If you want me to fix the bikes, I want to ride with you. Or I'm not doing it."

Razi started to laugh but the look on Mico's face stopped him in his tracks. He cocked his head to one side, his eyes narrowed into thin slits.

"You not joke," he said finally.

"No. I want to do more than repair bikes."

Razi stretched out the gum with his tongue, his expression thoughtful. After a few seconds he sucked it back in.

"You want in, you prove it." He jabbed a finger towards the tent. "See them. They all shown me they good. They got my back if I stuck. You understand?"

Mico wondered if the same rule had applied to Shakeel, but he kept quiet.

"Jump's on tonight," continued Razi. "Freight train coming through Tunnel. Me and the boys going. Come."

Mico hesitated. He had been to a jump a couple of months ago. It was suicide. Tens of men gambling with their luck and lives to throw themselves onto a train. He'd been too scared to try. Instead he'd stood and watched as the train arrived and others, braver than him, ran and leapt through the air. It had been like watching a strange kind of dance – a game between man and machine. As the last section of the train ran through the Tunnel, the men had become more and more desperate, some flinging themselves at the metal until their skin tore and bled. When Mico got back to the tent that night he'd been sick. Hassan had helped clean him up, but the smell had lingered on his clothes for days.

"What happen?" said Razi. "You scared?"

"No," said Mico quickly. He raised his voice a little, hoping he sounded confident. "I'll do it."

"Good." Razi punched him on the arm. "You do it, you in. Maybe we even jump. Then bikes no matter."

Mico forced a smile onto his face. Inside, he felt a little sick. There was a reason nobody ever made a jump. It was like trying to catch steam with your hands. Impossible unless you were ready to burn.

5

Darkness fell impossibly fast. As the last of the daylight dimmed, the butterflies that had been playing in Mico's stomach transformed into a tense knot. Razi had sent him back hours ago. "You run with me, you practise," he'd said.

Mico had spent all his time in the tent, staring at the blue of the tarpaulin. The thought of the train loomed at the back of his mind like a storm on the horizon. He would have liked some company but Hassan was still not back. When Sy had woken he'd tried talking to him.

"Do what you want," he replied, slinging his coat over his shoulder. He spoke with an accent, his words slow and weighty.

"You want to jump, jump. You want to stay, stay."

With that he had left for a game of dominoes. Mico had been cross at him until he'd realised that Sy was right. The decision was his. In truth, it had been easy to agree to Razi's challenge. He had that way with people. All it took was a smile and a wink and he'd have them eating out the palm of his hand. It wasn't just that he was smart. He knew how to stay alive. As if life was a game and winning was easy.

Mico would never forget his first few months in the camp. He'd never been away from home before and here he was, alone, on the other side of the world. To begin with he'd bunked with a family who'd arrived on the same boat as him. Two screaming kids and one silent mother. Some days after Razi offered him the bike job the woman's husband arrived. A fat man with no hair and crooked lips. He'd kicked Mico out the same day.

It was Razi who had found him space with Hassan and Sy. Sure, he'd docked three bikes' worth of food but it was that or go to the Ghost-Men. And once you started down that road you were inviting a whole heap of trouble. It was fine if you had the money to pay them back. If not... well, they had other ways of extracting their debts. "Favours", they called them. Could be simple stuff. Wash their clothes. Polish their boots. But if you were fast and smart they'd put you to work as their eyes and ears around the camp. It was all a question of policing. See, they didn't care if two men were fighting. But if one of those men had a weapon, a knife, say, then they wanted to know about it. Couldn't take the risk of someone slitting their throats at night.

But spying for the Ghost-Men was dangerous. Nobody likes a rat. If you were found out there was every chance you'd get beat. Razi had his own methods. Since setting up the bike racket he'd been dealing with the Ghost-Men directly. So long as he kept their palms greased they left him alone. Then he'd sit in a circle with his boys and cuss them till the air turned black. Mico had often seen them. Smoking or playing cards in the twilight. Just the thought of joining them made his heart sing.

Hassan arrived just as Mico was getting ready to leave. He had a small bowl in his hand and a big smile on his face.

"Got you and Sy a feast," he said. "Some sort of stew. Just don't ask me what's in it."

Mico didn't even look. His stomach was turning enough cartwheels already. He was certain he was going to be sick. Hassan stared at him.

"You OK?"

"I'm going to the jump."

"What?"

"There's a cargo train coming through tonight. Razi asked me to join him."

The smile dropped from Hassan's face.

"Don't be an idiot. You know how dangerous the jumps are." He spoke so fiercely that some stew slopped out of the bowl onto his shoes.

"Razi thinks he's untouchable but you should know better. Don't you remember what happened last time? Forget it, Mico. The Tunnel's no place for a kid."

It was the last thing he should have said. Mico stood up, his fists clenched.

"I'm nobody's kid. Not here. And you're not my mother. So lay off."

Hassan blinked, his face crumpling slightly as Mico brushed past him. He hadn't even reached Razi's before the guilt hit. Weeks before arriving at the camp Hassan had lost his little brother. He'd caught a fever while at sea. Hassan shouldn't have blamed himself but he did. That's why he was always on Mico's case.

For a moment, Mico thought about going back to

apologise. If anyone understood what that kind of loss felt like it was him. But he was in sight of Razi's tent now and there was Razi himself, parading about like a lord. He saw Mico coming and waved impatiently. Mico hurried forwards. Apologies would have to wait.

★ ✦ ★

Mico stared, wide-eyed, at the crowd of men around him. Some were huddled together in groups, praying, while others, like him, stood alone, their expressions fierce with intent. One caught him looking and gave him a thumbs up. Mico looked down at his shoes, embarrassed. For the hundredth time that evening, he wondered why he had come.

"All right, Mico?"

Razi appeared beside him and clapped him on the back. He caught the look on Mico's face and grinned.

"You scared?"

"I'm fine."

"Good. No fear, little man. You think, you fall. Too much thinking eat the brain. I run, I jump, easy. No sweat."

"How many have you done?"

"Five, almost."

"Almost?"

"Last jump too many people. Slow train, double hungry crowd. Hot tracks, hot mood." He brought his fist down onto his palm. "If I had stayed, I would be flat like a worm. Razi juice all over."

He laughed. Somehow, Mico couldn't bring himself to join in.

"What time's the train?" he asked.

31

Razi held up his wrist, face screwed in mock concentration as he inspected an invisible watch. He laughed again and punched Mico's arm.

"You worry like old man."

They were waiting by the tracks just outside the entrance to the Tunnel. The French authorities had recently put up fences to barricade the site, but Razi and his boys were men of resources. They always brought cutters with them.

"Move the blood. Get warm," said Razi, jumping up and down. "Train here soon."

Mico watched him in silence. Part of him still felt guilty about how he'd left things with Hassan. Razi prodded him in the chest.

"What I tell you? Jumping like music. You play good when you relaxed. See them?" He threw a hand out to a group of men who were praying. "They scared so they pray." He snorted. "No God here. Better to look at the train. Pick the spot, keep eyes on it. Run like cheetah. *Da-dum, da-dum.*" He pounded his fists in the air like he was beating a drum. "Like music, see. *Da-dum, da-dum, da-dum.*"

At that moment the air was torn apart by a piercing scream. Razi drew an excited breath and grabbed hold of Mico's sleeve.

"You ready?"

Before Mico could reply he was being pulled towards the tracks. The whistle grew louder. Razi was dancing like an electric wire. His eyes shone with exhilaration.

"We wait here," he explained. "Too close, not enough speed. Train comes, more space to run."

Mico nodded dumbly. Inside, he was a mess. Part of him wanted to back off now, before it was too late, but there was another bigger voice telling him to go for it. It was about more than Razi now. After what had happened at the Ghost-Men's tent, he had a point to prove. He had to know he wasn't a coward. And there was something else, something contagious about the energy of those around him. Maybe if he was fast enough he stood a chance of jumping the train. An express ticket direct to England.

Around him the men shuffled restlessly like soldiers preparing to go to war. The air crackled with anticipation. Hot and fierce like a firecracker. Then, with a great whooshing noise, the train was upon them.

They ran.

Shouts and yells erupted on either side of them. Battle cries. The men threw themselves forward as the train screeched along the rails. The air was filled with its smell. Metal against metal. It tasted black on Mico's tongue.

"Stay close," bellowed Razi.

The wind slapped Mico like a whip as he fought to stay alongside the older boy. He was only vaguely aware of his legs moving, of the ground retreating beneath his feet. He could feel Razi's arms pumping beside him. Hear the sharp in-out of his breath. Out of the corner of his eye, he saw the tail end of the train leave the Tunnel. It was going impossibly fast and yet they had only a few metres left to go now... three, two...

Suddenly, it was all over. Somebody piled into Mico, hard enough to make him stumble. He shouted, but his cry was instantly swallowed by thirty open mouths. The ground leered up to meet him. A dull pain shot through his shoulder, but all Mico was aware of was the noise. It was inside him, squeezing the blood from his bones. Feet against earth, earth against feet. Flesh bumping and thumping into each other.

He curled into a ball and threw his hands over his head, willing it to be over before someone stamped on him. All at once, a cheer rang out. Mico lifted his head a fraction. The train was ahead of them now and everyone was slowing. He staggered up onto his knees. The men in front of him were tall, but there was enough of a gap between them to see what all the excitement was about. Or rather, who.

Blood was smudged across his face and hands but there he was, smile flashing like a 100-watt bulb. Razi. Half of him was pressed up against the train, the other half jerking like a puppet doll as he fought to stay on. A rush of feeling surged through Mico as he watched him. He didn't know whether it was pride or disappointment, only that it hurt like a punch to the stomach.

Those watching put up their hands in salute. What came next was so quick that they were still saluting when it happened. One second, Razi was holding onto the train. The next, he was falling through the air. His mouth opened. Though he was far away, Mico was certain he heard a scream. Then the train leapt ahead and Razi slammed onto the concrete beside the tracks. His body twitched and was still. In the distance, the train let out a final whistle.

6

There was no funeral for Razi. As soon as the French authorities realised what had happened they took charge of his body and that was that. A week later, Hassan came into the tent with news.

"The government's furious," he said. "They're doubling the police guard around the Tunnel."

"What of Razi?" asked Sy without looking up. He was counting money on top of his coat. Mico wished he would stop. It felt disrespectful somehow. As if Razi's death was no more important than the weather.

"Are they flying him back to his family?"

"I don't know." Hassan looked tired as he spoke. "A proper send-off is the least he deserves." He sighed. "I guess it doesn't matter anymore. Wherever Razi is no government can touch him now."

But it mattered to Mico. He'd never forget the look on Razi's face as he was flung off the train; part surprise, part resentment as if he'd had a deal with life and life had cheated him at the last minute. It had all happened within seconds, but when Mico remembered it, everything seemed to pass in slow motion – the slap of Razi's body hitting the ground, the panic of the men as they ran forward, the blood pooling around his head.

If it had been someone else he knew what Razi would have said.

"Look at that. Messy mess. Clean it quick or tourists run away." Then he'd have laughed. Razi always found a reason to laugh. It was one of the things Mico would miss most about him.

That evening, when he was certain Hassan and Sy were asleep, he crept out of the tent towards the woods. Since he'd got back from the jump last week, Hassan had found some reason or another to stay with him. It had helped, especially those first few days after Razi's death, but now it was getting on his nerves. He needed some time alone. More than that, he still had to say goodbye to Razi. Hassan hadn't been at the jump. He didn't understand.

When he reached the first line of trees, Mico slowed. He inspected the ground in front of him, eyes straining in the gloom. The grass stank. There weren't enough toilets in the camp so when people were desperate they came here. He chewed on his lip. Maybe it would be better to come back in the morning. These trainers were the only pair he had.

But some things are better done under the cloak of night. And he owed it to Razi. Holding his breath, he inched forward. The trees grew thickly here. Sad and plain-looking, they watched his progress in stony silence. A chill breeze tickled his neck. Mico shivered. Esther had once told him a story about how trees were once people who had met with horrible deaths.

"They're ghosts, Mico," she'd said, holding a candle to her chin. "They can't leave the earth, see. Their souls bound to it like rope. But sometimes it happens that their souls get loose. And you better hope you're not walking past then. Because souls get awful lonely and if you're not careful, they'll reach out and grab you."

Mico had laughed then, but he was anxious now. What if Razi's soul was trapped in one of these trees? Who was to say he wouldn't jump out and grab Mico? After all, if Mico had kept up with him it would have been the two of them on that train. Maybe he wouldn't have died.

Mico shook his head.

"Don't be stupid," he whispered. It was all Esther's fault. She'd always loved frightening him. Out of the two of them she had always been the stronger one. If they dared each other to climb the baobab she'd always reach the highest branch. If they swam in the river she could always hold her breath the longest.

A familiar wave of pain flared inside him as he thought of the last time he'd seen her. She'd been outside on the veranda, helping Ma shell peas for dinner. Mico had been trying to unload a new batch of chickens. Every time he got near a cage, a beak would come out and nip his finger. By the time he was finished his entire hand had been covered in red bites. Esther had taken one look at him and exploded with laughter. He forced the memory back down. He would not think about her. He could not.

He was almost in the centre of the wood when he spotted what he was looking for. The flowers weren't much but they were the best he could do. As he drew closer, a thin shaft of moonlight broke through the clouds, illuminating the shiny blue of their petals. Mico picked a bunch of the nicest-looking ones. Then he made his way back to the camp. Though it was late, there were still some men drifting around. One leered towards him, babbling drunkenly in a foreign language. Mico swerved to avoid him and hurried towards the camp entrance.

Almost as soon as he was outside, he felt a great heaviness lift away from him. He inhaled deeply. The air was lighter here, easier to breathe. The camp sometimes felt like a great big waiting room. You were just *there*. Then, one day, if you were lucky, you might get away. If you didn't you'd probably end up like the Doctor. Or Razi. Mico wasn't sure which was worse.

From the entrance, he turned left then continued straight for a time until he reached an underpass. On the wall, somebody had scrawled a message in thick black lettering: *FRANCE IS DOG LIFE. ENGLAND GOOD LIFE.*

Mico barely gave it a second glance. He sped through the underpass then out onto another street. He hadn't gone far when he spotted two French officers approaching. He swore under his breath. It hadn't occurred to him that there might be patrols here. After Razi's death the government seemed to have clamped down everywhere. He stuffed the flowers into his jacket and bent his head low, hoping they wouldn't notice him. It didn't work.

"Hey! Hey, you! Stop there."

Mico trailed to a halt.

"Where are you going?"

The first officer was flabby and his English sounded wheezy and strained.

"For a walk."

"A walk? At this time?"

Mico nodded. He was aware that the second officer was staring at him. He hadn't said anything yet, but Mico could feel the suspicion rising off him, hot and stifling like steam from an iron.

"I needed some air," he said.

"Well, you've had it," replied the first one. "Go back to the camp."

"What are you carrying?"

The second officer's voice was as sharp as a knife.

"Nothing," said Mico, a fraction too quickly. The officer pursed his lips. Before Mico could protest, he reached forward and whipped open the corner of his jacket. The flowers dropped to the ground. The officers stared at them for a moment. Then the second one smirked.

"Meeting a girlfriend?"

"No."

"A boyfriend, then?"

Mico felt the blood rush to his cheeks.

"Jacques…"

"No, wait. I want to hear what he says."

"I told you already. I was going for a walk."

"Do you know what I think?"

The officer moved closer so that his face was pressed right up to Mico's. He had a little scar on his chin. Bristles of hair protruded out of his nose like a regiment of soldiers.

"I think you're lying."

He prodded Mico's chest.

"You know what happens to liars? They're punished."

He stepped forward onto the flowers. Mico watched

as the petals crumpled under the weight of his boots. A loud rushing noise rang through his ears. He opened his mouth to say something, but one look at the officer's face and he shut it again. He wasn't going to give him the satisfaction.

"Jacques. That's enough."

His partner spoke with quiet firmness. He looked at Mico. A trace of emotion, regret perhaps, flitted across his face then disappeared.

"Go back to the camp," he said.

Mico took one last look at the flowers. Then he turned and walked slowly away.

He did not run. Neither did he go back to the camp. He stopped in the underpass and sat against the wall to think. He still had a job to do and he wasn't going back until it was finished. He was fairly certain the officers wouldn't come this way. The police station was at the other end of town. He just had to wait for them to finish their patrol then he could go back and collect the flowers.

The underpass was cold. Mico blew on his hands and stuffed them into his armpits. It was difficult to imagine it would be summer in a few weeks. Summer had always been his favourite season. Summer was Ma's ginger-and-lime cordial. It was hot rains and dust and Uncle Abu's cigar on the front step.

What would they think if they saw him now? He had grown taller since his arrival in camp. The skin had sunk around his eyes and mouth. His hair was stretched back into a tight ponytail. Too loose and it collected the dirt. Hassan had often told him to get it cut, but he preferred it long. It made him appear tougher this way. He leant his head back against the wall and took a deep breath. He had been told to find a new life, a safer one. But nobody had warned him how hard that might be. Nobody had told him that in order to live, he'd have to give up everything he loved. Perhaps that was why he wanted to send Razi off properly. Goodbyes were important. They were a way of remembering.

After a while, Mico rose to his feet. The streets were silent. The flowers were lying where the officer had left them. He picked up the ones that were the least damaged. Then he stepped over the others and continued into the darkness.

7

The sea looks different at night. That was the first thought that struck Mico as he walked onto the beach. He had not been here often. Not since his arrival in port when he had been sick all over the Lizard's boots. Back then, the sea had glittered. Blue, bright and full of promise. Now it was black and threatening; wild.

Kneeling down, he brought out the flowers and laid them, stem by broken stem, across the water.

"Go in peace, Razi," he murmured. "Find a better place than this."

He waited a moment, half expecting some word of thanks, a whisper carried in the wind, but there was nothing. Mico watched in silence as the flowers floated away. Shakeel had come to see him earlier. The police had released him a couple of days ago. After Razi's death he'd quickly established himself as the new leader of the group. He'd turned up at the tent asking if Mico was still looking to work. Mico had turned him away. His heart just wasn't in it anymore.

Sighing, he lay back against the evening sky. Stars twinkled above him in arrogant silence. It was all right for them, thought Mico. Nobody could touch them up there. No-one could force them out of their homes, away from their family.

The stars had been out, too, on the night the men had come for the farm. For months, Uncle Abu had been speaking of growing unrest. A recent government corruption scandal had left a bitter taste in people's mouths. Word of rebellion floated between towns. Mico heard it all without interest. Politics was for adults. It meant nothing to him.

But nobody had told the rebels that.

By the time Mico awoke, the enclosure was already on fire. He had run out onto the veranda to be met by a giant wall of flames. The chickens screamed in wild fear. In the distance, the men with masks watched and cheered. Smoke coiled around their eyes like snakes.

The fire had grown like a monster, a fierce beast that spat and hissed with hunger. The men had stayed to watch for a while then they had driven away, gunshots cracking in celebration behind them. To this day, Mico did not know why they had come for the farm. It was jealousy, perhaps. Power.

Suddenly, he did not want to remember anymore. He sat up and splashed some water over his face as if somehow he could wash the memories away.

As he stood to leave there was a low shuffling beside him. A few metres away, someone was standing beside the water. Mico watched as the man wobbled on his feet. Even from that distance it was obvious he was drunk.

Mico was about to tell him to move away when

he saw the man's hand reach down to his trousers. Moments later, the air was filled with the unmistakeable trickle of piss. Mico stared in disgust. The man was doing it in the sea.

"Hey!"

Mico didn't even know how angry he was until he began shouting.

"Hey! What do you think you're doing?"

But the man was too drunk or too stupid to listen.

Mico stood up and stomped towards him.

"I'm talking to you. This is a public place. Go and do that somewhere else."

The man was zipping up his trousers. Only when he'd finished did he look up.

It was the Lizard.

"What is it, boy?"

His voice was slurred with drink.

"Can't a man do his business in peace?"

Mico should have left then. But he was angry, angry with the French officers, angry that Razi's flowers were now in the same water as the Lizard's piss.

"You're disgusting," he said.

The Lizard laughed. Snot exploded out of his nose onto his lips. He wiped it away with his hand and held his palm out to Mico.

"Come. I apologise."

Something in Mico snapped. With a brutish howl, he threw himself forwards. Slow with drink, the Lizard staggered and slipped back into the sea. Mico was on top of him in seconds. Without thinking, he forced the Lizard's face beneath the water. Reason had deserted him. All he wanted was to *hurt*.

They struggled. Man and boy. Thrashing beneath

the moonlight like two ancient creatures of the deep. Suddenly it was all over. Weak with effort, the Lizard dropped his arms. Realising that he was going to kill him if he didn't stop, Mico pulled him up. The Lizard spluttered, coughing water over them both. Then he giggled. Mico glared at him. The Lizard blinked stupidly. His eyes were empty and black. Where there should have been a soul there was nothing. The man really was a ghost.

Sickened, Mico rolled himself onto his feet. The scar on his shoulder throbbed like a brand. The Lizard had done that to him, that first day in port when he'd accidentally been sick over his shoes. Snake-tongue flicking in and out to the whip of his belt.

"Blue, bird, fish, fly," burbled the Lizard. "Sky, sink, sink, swim."

"You filthy drunk," muttered Mico. He stepped away and scooped handfuls of water onto himself to wash off the Lizard's stink. "It should have been you, not Razi."

The Lizard tilted his head. He scratched his crotch.

"Razi," he said, testing the name in his mouth. "Who's that? Your friend?"

Mico resisted the urge to push him back under. Even after doing business with him the Ghost-Man didn't remember Razi's name. Shivering a little, he bent down and pulled off the Lizard's shoes.

"That's for him," he said, tossing one into the sea. Then he threw the second. "And that's for my shoulder. Go fetch."

The Lizard wiggled his toes. He snorted with laughter. Mico took one last look at him before turning back to the camp.

45

8

It took three days for Mico's clothes to dry. His trainers took nearly twice as long. Hassan didn't seem to believe him when he said he'd slipped. He kept throwing Mico puzzled glances when he thought he wasn't looking. At last, one evening he cracked.

They were inside the tent. The day had started off warm but clouds had gathered in the mid-afternoon and it was now raining. The water hit against the tarpaulin like stones.

Sy drew his head up and scowled.

"This country is cursed," he declared.

"Your go," said Mico.

The two of them were playing dominoes. They'd been at it for ages. Mico didn't mind. It helped distract him from the growling in his stomach. Lunch today had been pasta, carrots, yoghurt and a hot dog. He'd planned to eat it slowly, maybe even save the yoghurt for dinner, but it was in his mouth and down his throat before he could stop himself. Tomorrow he hoped to do better.

"No beach today, eh, Mico," said Hassan, flicking a casual look at the T-shirt drying listlessly on the tent pole above them. "You can swim all you want out there."

Mico shuffled his dominoes harder than he needed to. One flew into the air and smashed down on the neat row already spread out across the floor. Sy made a noise of disapproval and began straightening the pieces.

"I told you," he said. "I went for a walk."

"Hm," said Hassan. Then, a second later, "You couldn't wait till the morning?"

"I needed to clear my head," said Mico steadily. He had been expecting Hassan to break a lot sooner and had prepared his answers already.

"How'd you fall?"

"*Sha*, Hassan," said Sy impatiently. "You ask too many questions. Leave him alone."

They were interrupted at that moment by the sound of feet outside. The sombre hum of men's voices drifted through the air, growing quieter as they passed by.

"They're trying tonight?" said Mico, swiftly using the distraction to steer the conversation away from himself.

"Maybe better," said Sy. "Police don't want to get wet so they stay inside."

"It's crazy," said Hassan. "Paying the Ghost-Men to smuggle you into a lorry is bad enough. Trying yourself is madness."

"Not madness," said Sy quietly. "These people have no choice. That is why they have travelled deserts and oceans. You think they come all that way to live in this dump? They have left one hell for another."

As he spoke, Mico heard his Ma wailing; he saw

47

Uncle Abu picking his way through the ashes of their home, a broken figure of a man. But he could not see Esther. He would never see her. How it had happened they could only guess. Perhaps she had been the first to see the flames. Perhaps she had run out to the enclosure, hoping to save the birds. Or perhaps she had been taken. In all the chaos nobody had noticed. And now she was gone, swallowed by the fire along with everything else.

"We all have," argued Hassan. "But risking your life every night isn't the answer."

"He's right," said Mico, putting another domino down. "Most of them get pulled off at the checkpoints anyway. It's a waste of time."

Sy shrugged.

"If I thought you were wrong I'd be out there with them. Once I get enough money I'll ask the Ghost-Men to arrange me a car." He laid his final domino onto the floor and smirked at Mico.

"Looks like I win."

A week later, and Mico's shoes were finally ready. He wriggled his toes pensively in the soles. If he pressed down hard enough he could feel an unpleasant damp-ness rising up to meet his skin. When he stood up, his feet felt extra bouncy like he was walking on sponges. But anything was better than the plastic bags he'd been using.

"You be all right?" asked Sy, poking his head through the tent's opening.

Mico bounced up and down on his feet. He grinned.

"I'm going to kick your ass."

Sy grunted and ducked back outside. "Hurry. We're late."

It was the last Sunday of the month and that meant football. Aside from money it was the only thing Sy cared about. Every month, he posted the notice on the signboard at the camp entrance. He organised the players and the match times. He'd even bartered a proper ball from one of the locals.

They played between the tents. It wasn't a huge pitch. The ground had hardened in deep ruts because of the rain but the players were always guaranteed a decent audience. The teams were haphazard, depending on how many turned up. Sy was always in charge. Mainly because he was the biggest and naturally commanded authority, but, more importantly, because he had the ball.

This afternoon's match was for Razi.

There were over twenty men already waiting when Sy and Mico arrived. Shakeel and the rest of the group. Others that Razi regularly did business with. A couple of beaten-down kids who Mico didn't recognise.

Sy motioned all of them together.

"Everyone, choose positions. I want midfielders here—" He pointed to his right then moved his hand in an arc through the air. "Strikers, defence…"

As the players shuffled amongst themselves, Mico glanced to the row of tents on his left. Sure enough, the Doctor was sitting on a chair with a red-and-white football scarf tied around his neck. He never missed a match.

Mico raised his hand.

The Doctor beamed and waved back with such enthusiasm that he almost toppled off his chair. Hassan was there too. He didn't really understand the game

49

and Mico felt a rush of affection for him as he caught the confusion on his face. Hopefully the Doctor would explain the rules.

He felt a tap on his shoulder.

"We're ready," said Sy. "I've told them no fouls or they're out. You all right playing midfield?"

Mico shrugged.

"Whatever. Shall I start or sub?"

"You start," said Sy. "I'll switch you later."

The match began well for Mico's team. Less than ten minutes in and they were already up two goals. By half-time, Mico had been subbed twice and the other team had managed to level it up.

"Come on, Mico!" shouted the Doctor from the side-lines as they took their positions for the second half. "Do it for Crawley!"

Mico sprinted forward as the ball was put into play. He went for a tackle, missed, watched the ball cross over into the box. The pass was poor, however, and landed by a defender.

"Here!" yelled Mico, throwing his arm into the air. The defender looked up, noted Mico's position and booted the ball towards him. Mico took it on his right foot and dribbled forward. This was their chance.

"Go, Mico!"

The Doctor's voice carried across to him on the air. Mico glanced up for a pass and that's when he saw her. A little way ahead a girl was walking through the line of defenders towards him. She was wearing a stripy blue dress over leggings. A yellow rucksack was slung across her back.

He hesitated. Couldn't she see they were playing? Suddenly the girl raised her arms and flashed him a smile. Mico looked down at his feet in realisation. She wanted him to pass the ball.

At that moment, one of the defenders, a young rabbit-faced boy, became aware of her presence. Annoyance twisted across his features. Stepping forward, he took hold of the girl's rucksack and started to drag her away. With a cry of outrage, she twisted free and kicked him between the legs. The boy howled and dropped to the floor.

"Foul!" bellowed the Doctor. "Off, off!"

"Leila!"

An older, pregnant woman came lumbering through the defenders. She was holding a case in one hand and a water bottle in the other. With a withering glance at the boy on the floor, she took hold of the girl's collar and pulled her off the pitch towards the tents. They were not yet out of view when the girl turned and looked at Mico.

He could have sworn she winked.

9

"Leila and Aysha," declared Hassan triumphantly as he entered the tent that evening. Mico was doing push-ups.

"Who?" he wheezed.

Hassan sat down and started to take off his shoes.

"The pair that interrupted your match. They arrived this morning." He glanced at Sy's empty space.

"He's gone out," said Mico, resting against the floor. "Said Omar had found him a job. Old lady needs her fence repaired. They've gone to take a look at it."

He huffed as he lifted himself into the air. Sy hadn't asked if he wanted to come. He wasn't the sharing type. Didn't matter what it was; words or money, he liked to keep both to himself. The only reason he stuck with Omar was because Omar spoke French. And he had a fox's nose for sniffing out work.

"Did he say when he'll be back?" asked Hassan, sliding his shoes under his pillow. Like Mico, he too had only the one pair. They were the lucky ones. Those who were less fortunate wandered around in broken flip-flops.

"No. Late, probably."

Hassan frowned. Mico knew what he was thinking. Lately, they'd heard rumours. Of a group wandering the streets at night. Men with time to kill and more anger than was good for them. They wore masks and carried sticks. Maybe some were police, maybe not. Either way they'd come out hungry, looking to hunt. In all the grey of that city there was only one jungle. Boys, men, they weren't picky; if you were from the camp, you were enough.

"Relax," said Mico. "Sy can look after himself."

Hassan tried to smile.

"Yeah, you're right."

But he still sounded worried. Mico sat up, his arms aching.

"How'd you find out their names?" he said, deciding to change the subject.

"Sara went to visit them this afternoon," said Hassan. "They're a few tents away from her. Aysha was asleep, but she talked to the younger one. Leila. They're sisters."

"Where they from?"

"Egypt, I think."

"Why'd they leave?"

"Sara didn't say."

"Did she ask?"

Hassan shrugged.

"Does it matter? We're all here now. Who cares why? It's where we want to go that's important."

Something about this statement didn't ring true to Mico, but he said nothing. Instead he turned over onto his back and began sit-ups.

"You should go and introduce yourself," said Hassan.

"Why?"

"It'll give you something to do. And you might have stuff in common with Leila."

"Like what?"

"I don't know. I thought it might give you something to do. In case you're bored."

"What—" puffed Mico, "makes – you – think – I'm – bored?"

Hassan smiled unexpectedly.

"Nothing," he said.

✭ ✭ ✭

Mico ignored Hassan's advice. He didn't need friends. What he wanted was to get to England. But that was looking less and less likely. Since the increase in police patrols the Ghost-Men had upped their prices. And he couldn't bring himself to jump another train, not yet.

One morning he tried asking Sy if he could go with him to repair the fence.

"Why?" asked Sy.

"I need money."

"I thought you were helping Shakeel's lot."

"No." Mico paused, thinking about Razi. He shrugged. "They don't pay me in cash."

Sy didn't look convinced.

"I'm strong," continued Mico earnestly. "And good with my hands. I could help you."

"No."

"Why not?"

"I don't want your help," said Sy. "And I can't pay you. You want work you find it yourself."

He was gone before Mico could think of a suitable reply.

The next few days passed quietly. Sy left early in the morning and returned before dusk. Hassan got a haircut in exchange for two magazines. Mico spent most of his time walking about the camp. A church and a mosque had recently been built so he often saw families heading off to pray. Men boiled tea on a stove. Others sat hunched over the ground, playing a game of dice. Mico had no idea of the rules, only that it involved a lot of shouting and back-slapping. He was not invited to join them, however, so he continued on his way.

Only once did he see the Lizard. To his disappointment he was wearing a new pair of shoes.

He did not meet Leila again until a week later. He was with the Doctor, trying to fix his chair; after the excitement of the recent football match it had somehow lost a leg. The Doctor wasn't much help. Aside from commenting on how quickly his nephew Amir would have done it, he merely sat and watched him.

After a couple of hours – and a dozen splinters – Mico was close to giving up. He was about to suggest that a three-legged chair might work just fine, when, suddenly, the air exploded with a cry of indignation. A figure came streaking past the tents on their left. Mico didn't have to look too closely to see who it was. Leila's yellow rucksack was bouncing like a wild monkey on her back.

"Ai! Give it back, girl."

Leila screeched to a stop and wheeled around to face her pursuer, a thin, bearded strap of a boy.

"That's my bike."

Mico could see why he'd chased after it. The bike was one slick pair of wheels. As red as the devil and almost brand-new. He wondered where Shakeel had got hold of it.

"So? It's mine now."

The boy put his hands on his hips.

"It's not for girls. You might hurt yourself."

"Yeah?"

Leila leant backwards slightly and lifted the bike clean in the air, balancing on the back wheel. The boy's mouth dropped.

"Watch this, *y'kalb.*"

She pedalled towards him. The front wheel of the bike hung suspended in the air like an open jaw. The Doctor laughed. Then it all went horribly wrong. The bike went over a rough patch and Leila panicked. Too late, she tried to right her balance. But the back wheel wobbled, gave way. Both bike and girl crumpled onto the ground.

"No!"

The boy's howl stabbed the air like glass.

"Look what you've done."

Something, a stone perhaps, had cut the bike's front tyre. The boy rushed forward and gathered the wheel in his hands.

"This is your fault," he shouted, turning on Leila. "I swapped my radio for this. How am I going to fix it now?"

Leila sat up and brushed down her sleeves. Her lip was bleeding. The boy watched her expectantly. She spat some blood onto the ground. Cautiously, she poked a finger into her mouth.

"Think I lost a tooth," she said.

The boy glared at her.

Leila spat out some more blood.

This was too much for him. With a wild, wordless yell, he threw himself on top of her. A cloud of dirt exploded into the air as the two of them wrestled. Together, they were one kicking, spitting ball of fury; and for a moment, Mico was unable to distinguish girl from boy, boy from girl. It was not much different from a fight he had once seen on the chicken farm. Leila was stronger than he had expected, but the boy was heavier and angrier.

"He's going to kill her," murmured the Doctor as the boy began beating Leila's head against the dirt. A thin line of blood snaked along her cheek and dripped onto the ground.

"Hey!" said Mico. He stood up, flexing the chair leg in his hand. "She's had enough."

The boy glanced up at him then back down to Leila. The left side of her face was smudged with swirls of red and brown. His shoulders sagged. Perhaps it had just occurred to him that there was nothing manly about hitting a girl; or perhaps it was the realisation that doing so wouldn't bring his bike back.

"Where you going?" said Leila as the boy stood up. Her voice was all bent out of shape. She tried again. "Finish it."

The boy took one last look at her. Then he picked up his bike and wheeled it silently away. Leila lay there for a few moments. Finally, she sat up.

The rucksack made her appear younger, but up close, Mico could see she was almost the same age as him. Her hair had been tugged loose by the fight; an inky-black tangle now cascaded across her face in wild abandon. An ugly bruise was starting to darken above one eye, but the other glinted a fierce shade of brown – defiant and moody like the edge of a sunset.

"You all right?" he asked.

Leila glared at him through one eye.

"I could have taken him," she said. "Why'd you open your big mouth?"

"Why'd you steal his bike?"

Even with half her face mashed up, Leila managed to look unimpressed.

"It was his own fault. He shouldn't have whistled at me." She winced as she touched the side of her head. "Did you see his face? Like a rat's ass. He needed to be taught a lesson."

Mico stared at her.

"A good fight, yes," said the Doctor. "You punch him hard, hm?"

For the first time, a glimmer of a smile appeared on the girl's face.

"Best fighter in my street," she said proudly. Then she dabbed the blood under her nose and sniffed.

"No point fighting round here," said Mico. "You'll only make it harder for yourself."

"Maybe," sniffed Leila again. With some difficulty, she managed to wobble to her feet. "Maybe not."

10

They wouldn't become proper friends until nearly a month later. But before that came the other things.

The first was a new fence around the Tunnel. Mico went to see it with Hassan. It was a beast of a structure, towering high above them in a menacing show of steel. For days it remained the sole talking point in the tent. Of the three of them it was Sy who seemed the most affected by it. Mico had never seen him so angry.

"First the police patrols. Now this. What do they want? That we stay here and rot?"

"Relax, Sy," said Hassan. His reaction had been decidedly more positive. He saw the fence as a sign that the authorities had finally decided to sit up and take notice of them.

"The government just want to make sure nobody else gets killed. Don't you see? They're finally taking action. It's better than pretending we don't exist. They can't be passive anymore. They have to help us."

Sy snorted in disbelief. His face shone with a manic energy.

"Listen to yourself, Hassan. Do you hear what's coming out your mouth? The only action the government has taken is put up another barrier. They don't care about us. If they did, we wouldn't be living like this."

He was almost shouting.

"The Ghost-Men have already doubled their prices. Now it'll be triple."

"You need to calm down," said Hassan, placing a hand on Sy's shoulder.

Sy stepped backwards like he'd been stung.

"Don't touch me," he said.

Hassan's face twisted. His arms dropped to his sides. Mico looked from one to the other, conscious of the tension fizzing between them. He had never seen them like this before.

Sy turned and stormed out of the tent. Hassan inhaled sharply and sat down on the floor.

"What was that about? Hassan?"

"Doesn't matter."

"But—"

"Leave it, Mico."

Hassan lay down and turned his face away from him. "Please."

Over the coming days, Hassan and Sy went out of their way to avoid each other. The atmosphere in the tent was as hot as a rocket, fully charged and ready to explode. The evenings were the worst. Before the fight the three of them had killed time playing games. Dominoes, cards, something called *carrom* which Hassan had taught them using pebbles and plastic cups. Sometimes, Sy would get the ball out and they'd take turns throwing it to one another. It seemed strange, but

60

those moments had made Mico feel safer somehow. For a time, he'd been able to forget the world that was waiting outside to swallow him up.

Now, Sy and Hassan wouldn't even look at each other. If they had anything to say they'd say it through Mico. "Tell Sy that Omar was looking for him." "Tell Hassan to keep his stuff out my space." It was driving Mico crazy.

At last, in desperation, he went to visit Sara. She and Hassan were good friends; maybe he'd have spoken to her. At the very least, she'd listen. He'd already tried going to the Doctor, but he'd been shooed away. "Don't pull me into your problems, yes," the Doctor had said. "Young people. Hah! You only know how to fight."

It didn't occur to Mico that Sara might have problems of her own.

As he drew up to her tent, it was the Lizard's voice he heard first. Then Sara's, loud enough to make him pause. Sara was always so softly spoken. He had never heard her shout before.

Before he could turn back, the Lizard stumbled out. Sara followed.

"I've told you once," she said. "And I'll tell you again. No. Now leave."

The Lizard grabbed hold of her waist and pulled her close. Sara shoved him in the chest, but he was too strong. As she struggled to free herself he brought his mouth to her ear. Mico saw his lips moving and Sara's face twisting. She looked like she was about to cry.

He saw other things too. The way Sara held herself, stiff and scared, the Lizard's fingers gripping her top. A wave of fury rushed through him.

61

"Hey!" he shouted, starting forwards. "Let go of her."

The Lizard glanced his way. His gaze lingered a moment on Mico, sizing him up. With an amused smile, he released Sara and stepped up to meet him.

"What is it, boy? You got something to say?"

Mico noticed the Lizard's hand draw to his belt. He faltered, remembering the sting of the leather. Sara shook her head at him.

"Well?"

"No."

"No, sir."

Mico gritted his teeth, his fingers clenching round the knife in his pocket. It wouldn't take much. But if he accidentally missed his mark, the Lizard certainly wouldn't. He'd whip him for sure. And he'd take the knife. Without it, Mico would have nothing to protect himself.

"Say it. No, sir."

"No, sir," said Mico, his face burning with shame.

The Lizard moved up towards him and put a hand under his chin. His skin felt scaly and cool.

"Good."

He tilted Mico's head up.

"What's your name, boy?"

Mico thought back to that night under the stars. The night he'd had the Lizard at his mercy. The night he'd let him go.

"Mico," he said.

The Lizard raised an eyebrow and drummed his fingers against his belt. His face was as hard as an old boot.

"Mico, sir," said Mico. He could feel the Lizard stamping his face into his memory, but he forced himself to hold his gaze. He wasn't going to let him think he was scared.

62

"Mico." The Lizard repeated his name as if it left a bad taste in his mouth. "Didn't your mother teach you nothing? When adults talk, you don't interrupt. You keep quiet. Understand?"

Mico nodded. A tide of rage crashed inside him but he pushed it down. Today was not the day for a fight. The Lizard smiled and lightly slapped his cheek. Then he turned back to Sara.

"Think on what I said. I get you and your boy to England in a week. I don't ask for much in return."

Sara squared her shoulders.

"I'd rather die."

"Maybe. But what about your son?"

Sara's face dropped then, all the fight gone from her. The Lizard smirked.

"I'll come again. Maybe you change your mind."

He swung on his heels and walked away. Sara spat on the ground after him. An angry red flush was spreading across her neck.

"I'm sorry you had to see that," she said, turning back to Mico. She was a small woman, thin, with slender arms and legs. Before arriving at the camp she had been a lecturer at a university. Her face was like a doll's, smooth and pretty with a dainty mouth.

Mico did not ask her what the Lizard had wanted. He'd seen enough to guess.

"Are you all right?" he asked.

Sara forced a smile onto her face.

"I can handle myself. It's Tamal I worry about. If he'd seen—" Her lips tightened. "Hassan's taken him to the library."

The library was a small charity-run shack at the far end of the camp. There were never enough books to go round but the volunteers kept a special section for the kids, picture books, funny stories, comics – stuff to make them laugh so they didn't forget how.

She sighed and smoothed the folds of her dress.

"Hassan must have told you. Tamal keeps asking about his father. Every morning he wakes up and takes me to the front of the camp. Says he doesn't want his *abba* to get lost finding us." She pressed her lips together. "I should tell him the truth. That's what Hassan says. But Tamal has enough to deal with already. He still doesn't understand why we're here. I have tried explaining but he is a child. War means nothing to him. If I tell him the truth about his father it will break his heart. He always loved him the most."

Mico did not know what to say. Hassan had told him about Sara's husband. He'd followed his family on a separate boat, but the vessel had developed a fault and sank. There hadn't been any survivors.

He shuffled his feet awkwardly.

"They'll probably be a while yet," said Sara, mistaking his embarrassment for impatience. "You're welcome to come in and wait for him."

Mico followed her inside. The tent was clean, but sparse with precious little furniture. It made Mico's heart ache just to look at it.

On one side a photo had been tacked to the wall. It showed Sara holding Tamal. His mouth was smothered with chocolate. Next to them stood a handsome man, his arm swung carelessly across Sara's shoulder. All three of them were laughing.

"Tamal's tenth birthday," said Sara, following Mico's gaze. "It was the last one we celebrated together." She was silent for a moment. Mico wished he hadn't come.

Sy and Hassan's argument seemed silly compared to what Sara was going through.

"I'm sorry there's nowhere for you to sit."

"I'm fine," said Mico quickly. "Actually, it was you I came to see. I wanted to speak to you about Hassan."

"Why? What's happened?"

"He's…" Mico faltered. "Him and Sy had a fight. They're not talking."

Sara looked puzzled.

"I'm not sure how I can help."

"I thought you could have a word with Hassan. He—" Mico blushed. "He cares about you."

"Oh, Mico."

Sara looked suddenly sad.

"Hassan knows his own mind. I am not as important to him as you think."

"You can still try. Please."

"I don't think it will help, but…" Sara shrugged. "If you really want me to."

"Thank you," said Mico. He hesitated. Sara waved her hand in the air.

"Don't worry. I won't mention you. Now—" She turned towards the back of the tent. "You are a guest in my house. And guests must be fed."

Before Mico could refuse, she thrust a bar of chocolate at him.

"Take it."

"No, I'm fine," said Mico, backing away.

"I'm not asking."

"Keep it for Tamal."

"He hates chocolate. Just like his *abba*."

"Then keep it for yourself."

Sara stepped forward, shaking the chocolate threateningly at him.

"I'm not asking, Mico. I might have left everything else behind, but I am still my mother's daughter. And she would never let a guest leave our house hungry."

Before Mico could protest, she forced the chocolate into his hands and pushed him out of the tent.

"Go now. I have work to do."

11

If Sara did speak to Hassan it made no difference. The friction in the tent remained, thick and bitter like smoke. A week later it got worse.

Sy's friend, Omar, went out in the evening to finalise another job. Almost ten men had been attacked in the last fortnight but Omar didn't seem to care. He walked those streets like he owned them. That was probably why they picked him.

When he returned the following morning he could hardly walk. They'd hit him so badly behind the knees that all you could see was the bruises. His face was even worse. It reminded Mico of the world map that Mr Bancho had pinned on the wall behind his desk. A squiggly mess of green lines and purple shades.

The doctors at the clinic looked Omar over and prescribed him two weeks of rest. He was lucky, they said. It was a miracle nothing had broken. But while he recovered, Sy was stuck in the tent. Out of work and out of temper. One morning, Mico asked if he wanted to play football. Turned out Sy had sold it.

"I'm not here to play games," he said. "You remember that."

With Sy brooding like a caged panther in the tent, it was no surprise Hassan spent most of his time outside. He'd even joined French classes. At the end of the camp was a makeshift classroom where the lessons took place. They were run by volunteers and held under a large sheet of tarpaulin strung up on a crooked tree trunk. At the front of the class was a chalkboard dotted with cartoon pictures of simple French words. A month after arriving in camp, Mico had tried the classes himself. He'd soon given up. Learning French was like hitting his head against a brick wall. In any case, he wouldn't have any use for it in England.

Some nights later, Hassan returned in a foul mood. Mico was lighting a candle when he entered. It was dangerous having fire so close to the tarpaulin but they didn't have much choice. Torches were hard to come by and expensive to maintain.

Without a word, Hassan kicked off his shoes and threw himself onto the floor. Mercifully, Sy wasn't in. He'd gone to see Omar.

"How was class?" asked Mico.

"How do you think?"

"It's French. What did you expect?"

"I don't know. I didn't think it would be so hard."

"Why are you bothering anyway? If it's an excuse to avoid Sy—"

"It's not," snapped Hassan. His eyes were red and swollen. He looked like he hadn't slept properly for days.

"But what's the point of learning French? You want to go to England. You said English films are getting bigger."

"I know what I said. But I'll start going mad if I carry on like this."

"Like what?"

"Like *this*." Hassan threw his hands into the air. For a moment he looked like a bird, flapping its wings against an invisible cage.

"I need to do something, Mico. The classes help me feel I've got a purpose in life. That's all."

"What about Sy?"

The words were out of Mico's mouth before he could stop them. Hassan stiffened.

"Are you still mad at him?"

Hassan didn't look like he was going to answer. Then he shook his head.

"I was never cross with Sy. It's this place. It makes everything seem so hopeless. Sy's scared. We all are, in our different ways. He just won't admit it."

"Well, maybe he should. I'm sick of watching him mope around."

Hassan looked at him then, really looked. It might have been the flicker of the candlelight, but Mico had never seen him so unhappy.

"We're all afraid of being fenced in," said Hassan quietly. "Sy is afraid because he thinks he's losing control over his life. He fears he won't be able to get away. But running isn't always the answer."

"What do you mean?"

"Ah, Mico." Hassan lay down on his back. "I'm tired. Let's talk about this another time."

Mico was silent for a few seconds. But there was something else bothering him.

"What about Omar? Who do you think attacked him?"

Hassan sighed.

69

"I don't know," he said eventually. "But I pity them. All that hate they're carrying around. Think how hopeless their own lives must be."

"Can't be any worse than ours," said Mico pointedly.

Hassan made no reply.

"Do you think it was the police?" A vision of an officer with a scar on his chin rose up from the edges of Mico's memory.

"I hope not," said Hassan. He yawned. "So many questions tonight, eh?" A sly grin spread across his face. "But you haven't said. How's that friend of yours? Leila?"

"She's not my friend."

"No?"

Hassan's grin widened.

"Then you're a fool. There's plenty of things can kill a person in this world. Loneliness is the worst."

Mico snorted and snuffed the candle between his fingertips.

"Stick to French, Hassan. You're a rubbish poet."

In reply, a cushion came flying at him through the gloom.

12

The next couple of weeks passed slowly. Sy moped. Hassan's French got a little better. In the evenings he'd sit outside and Mico could hear him muttering under his breath. *Bonjour, je m'appelle, bonjour.*

Some days, Mico kept the Doctor company. Once or twice, he visited Sara. She'd started an English class for the camp's youngest children; basic stuff like sounds and the alphabet. About fifteen of them would sit on the ground and practise. Mico had offered to help, but the kids all sat with their mums anyway so he wasn't really needed.

One morning, he tried teaching Tamal how to play chess. It had been his uncle's favourite game and Mico had played with him often. But it's difficult to teach chess to a ten-year-old, more so when the board is drawn in the dirt with a stick. After five minutes, Mico gave up and Tamal scampered off to find a more interesting game to play.

"He's stopped asking about his father," said Sara, raising one hand over her eyes as she watched him go.

"Before, I'd hear the question every few hours. Now, once a day."

"Isn't that a good thing?" said Mico, standing up.

"Is it?"

Sara's voice was hollow.

"With each day we stay, my son forgets his father. And you tell me that is a good thing?"

"I only meant—"

"Yes, I know."

There was an awkward silence.

"I'm sorry," said Sara shortly. She drew her arms across her chest. "I'm not sure if Hassan's told you, Mico. I've applied to stay in France."

Mico stared at her.

"I thought you wanted to go to England."

"If I was on my own, perhaps…"

She trailed off, wistful. Suddenly she reminded Mico of a little girl.

"Yesterday, he paid me another visit." She didn't need to say who. "Soon he will lose patience. I have Tamal to think about. It's not just his safety that worries me. Children have short memories. By the time we leave, will he even remember his father? When he thinks of his home will it be these tents he sees?"

Mico said nothing. How could he admit to her that faces were the first thing you forgot? That everything he had ever read in books was false. That memories never stayed still. They wavered and twisted and betrayed you, no matter how much you loved someone.

He could offer Sara no comfort, only lies.

72

The next day, Mico didn't feel like seeing anyone. Since yesterday, he'd been replaying his conversation with Sara over and over in his head. Not for the first time he wondered if he had been right to leave home. Should he have stayed? Tried to help rebuild? To look after Ma? The morning after the fire she had slumped down onto the blackened earth as if she would never rise again. No matter how hard Mico tried she would not move. Grief had settled upon her like a sickness. At last, Uncle Abu had to carry her away.

For some days they had stayed with friends. Reports of looting and violence blared across the news. Fear smothered the country like a blanket of ash.

When Uncle Abu had told Mico his decision, Mico had refused. He would not leave them. Nor his home. But Uncle Abu would hear no argument. He had lost one member of his family already. He would not lose another.

Shortly after the fire, he'd arranged for Mico to be taken to the port. He had given him a little cash, enough to purchase passage onto a boat. "You must build a new life for yourself," he'd said. "A better one. Somewhere you can stay without fear." Then he'd pulled Mico into a tight hug.

"You will have to be strong. Strong like your sister."

His hair had smelled of wood and smoke.

Wood and smoke.

That was how Mico would remember him all those months later.

He stayed in the tent for most of the afternoon, glad for a chance to be alone. Omar was finally being discharged so Sy was at the clinic. Hassan had gone to queue up for lunch.

73

After a while Mico grew tired of waiting for him to come back. Slipping his knife into his pocket, he headed outside. A couple of shops had recently popped up in the centre of the camp. They were little more than shacks really, with a limited choice of food and drink. Mico usually ignored them. No point looking if you had no money. But today the sight of all that food was too much to bear. Last night he'd finished off the chocolate that Sara had given him. That had been hours ago.

Shoving his hands in his pockets, he strolled over to the nearest shack. If he was lucky, one of the shop-keepers might take pity on him.

A fat man sat behind the first counter. He was wedged onto the tiniest of stools, skin drooping over it like a pancake. Though it wasn't a hot day, his forehead glistened with sweat.

"Ey," he said as Mico approached. He picked up a Pepsi and held it out to him.

"For free?" asked Mico hopefully.

The man snorted and put the can back on the counter.

"I can pay tomorrow."

"No. Today. Now."

"How much for the crisps?"

This next question came not from Mico, but Leila who had suddenly materialised beside him. The shop-keeper removed a flannel from his pocket and dabbed his head.

"Five euros."

"For one packet? That's extortion."

"You want it, you pay."

Leila appeared to consider this. The bruise around her eye had almost faded. After a moment, she shrugged and opened her rucksack.

"Fine. Give me the salted ones."

With an enormous draw of breath, the shopkeeper swivelled around. Quick as a flash, Leila grabbed two cans of Pepsi and stuffed them into her rucksack. She slung it back onto her shoulder and winked at Mico.

So she *had* recognised him.

"There," said the shopkeeper, throwing the crisps onto the counter. "Two euros."

Leila didn't even blink.

"Actually I've changed my mind. I'm not hungry anymore."

With a final smirk in Mico's direction, she sauntered coolly away. The shopkeeper's eyes narrowed in suspicion. His gaze moved from Leila back to the counter. A sudden look of understanding twisted across his flabby cheeks.

"Ey," he shouted. "You – girl!"

Leila didn't bother turning back. She started to run.

"You," said the shopkeeper, turning to Mico. His eyes were bulging so much they looked like they were going to pop out of his head.

"You helped her."

"No, I didn't," said Mico indignantly.

"Liar," said the man, lunging forward to make a grab for him. Mico ducked and ran.

"Oi! Come back!"

Mico didn't stop until he was among the tents. Panting hard, he bent down to recover his breath. He was lucky the shopkeeper had been so fat. As for Leila—

"You're not a bad runner."

Mico looked up. Leila was sitting against one of the

75

tents watching him. She had an open can of Pepsi in her hand.

He glared at her.

"You're a rubbish thief."

Leila had the grace to look offended.

"I didn't get caught, did I?"

"You got lucky."

"I don't believe in luck."

When Mico didn't reply, Leila took a swig from the can and held it out to him.

"Here," she said. "You earned it. Thanks for keeping your mouth shut."

Mico held her gaze a moment before taking the can from her. The liquid was warm, but sweet. He downed it in one. Then he grinned.

"You should have seen his face," he said, wiping his mouth with the back of his hand. "I thought his eyes were going to burst."

"Ey," said Leila, cocking her head in a perfect imitation of the shopkeeper. "Ey. What you doing? Thief. Ey."

Mico laughed.

"That's not bad."

They looked at each other, suddenly shy. Mico thought back to what Hassan had said. He didn't know if he was lonely or not. But friend was a dangerous word. Permanent, unlike everything in the camp.

Leila stood up.

"I should go," she said. "My sister will be waiting for me."

A stab of pain twisted in Mico's chest. Leila didn't know how lucky she was. Sure, he had Hassan and Sy, but they were just the guys he shared a tent with. They weren't family.

Leila hitched her rucksack onto her shoulders. Then she threw him a sly glance.

"I'll see you outside the camp tomorrow morning."

She was gone before Mico could ask why.

13

The next morning, Mico was up early. Dawn was just breaking over the horizon as he stepped out into the camp. The sky was pierced in shards of orange and pink, illuminating the tents in a faint glow of light. They looked sad and decrepit, hunchbacked beggars stooped against the dirt.

He passed hardly anyone as he walked. Everywhere was quiet. As he caught sight of the shops, he tensed then relaxed when he saw they weren't open. The front of the camp was empty. For one horrible second, Mico wondered if Leila had been messing with him. Maybe this was her idea of a joke. Then he spotted her sauntering towards him, rucksack fixed to her back.

She was built like a rubber band, small with wiry limbs. Her hair was like a mane. Thick, black curls twisted like vines around her face. She broke into a smile as she saw him.

"Hey. You're here."

For a moment she looked relieved. Then her expression shifted.

"Hope you don't scare easy," she said, sidestepping him with unmistakeable arrogance.

"Why? Where are we going?" asked Mico, following her onto the pavement.

"Not far."

"Are you going to tell me what we're doing?"

"You'll see."

Mico wasn't sure if he was supposed to feel annoyed or curious.

"What's in the rucksack?" he asked finally.

Leila stuck out her chin a little.

"Nothing."

"Nothing?"

"That's right."

Mico stopped, forcing Leila to a halt.

"If you don't trust me, there's no point in me coming. I might as well go back."

Leila turned and looked at him, her eyes hardening into thin slits. Mico held her gaze without flinching. He must have done something right because a couple of seconds later she nodded.

"It's my sketchbook," she said, walking again.

"That's what you're always carrying?"

Mico couldn't hide the surprise from his voice. Leila shrugged.

"It's important."

"So you like drawing?"

"Painting." A gleam appeared in Leila's eyes as she spoke. "One day, my paintings are going to be sold all around the world. But only to galleries. I don't want my work shut up in a rich person's house where nobody else can see it. It has to be for everyone."

She removed a squashed toffee from her pocket, bit off one dusty half, and handed the rest to Mico.

"What do you like?"

Mico threw the toffee into his mouth, wincing at the hardness of the caramel.

"I don't know," he said. It had been so long since anyone had asked him anything about himself he couldn't even remember.

"I want to go to college."

"To do what?"

"I don't know. Engineering, maybe." He shrugged. "I'm good at fixing things."

Leila made a face.

"Sounds boring."

"So does painting."

Leila shoved him in mock indignation. A short while later, she pulled him into a narrow street. They'd gone about halfway down when she abruptly stopped. They were standing beside a neat-looking house. It had a pretty garden; the pathway leading up to the door was cleanly swept and lined with flowers.

"Let's try this one," said Leila, crouching down behind the front wall. She motioned him to join her.

Mico was hit by a sudden jolt of alarm.

"We're not going to rob it, are we?" he said, kneeling beside her.

Leila glared at him.

"Course not. I just want to see who lives there, that's all."

"Why?"

From her pocket, Leila removed a bar of chocolate. A pang of hunger stabbed through Mico's stomach.

"Where'd you get that?"

"From one of the bibs. I queue up every morning to make sure I get something for my sister. You saw her at the match."

"Bibs?"

"You know, the charity lot. I always get extra because I'm short. They think I'm a child." She waved the chocolate in the air. "Here's the deal. Me and you are going to guess who lives in that house. Then one of us will knock on the door. Whoever gets it right gets the chocolate."

"That's stupid. What if we get caught? We're not kids."

"We're not invisible either," argued Leila. "But these people walk past the camp like we're not even there. I've seen them. They're embarrassed to look because they know it's wrong. Nobody should have to live like we do. It's not *right*."

Her voice was fierce but there was a vulnerability in her expression which caught Mico off-guard.

"You don't have to prove anything," he said gently. "We can just share the chocolate."

Leila didn't even appear to hear him.

"Look, I'll show you," she said. "It's not that hard."

Before Mico could stop her, she was strolling up the drive. He watched as she rang the bell, banged the letterbox then sprinted back towards him.

"Are you crazy?" he hissed as she threw herself down. Leila grinned.

"Wait for it."

Mico licked his lips. His heart thudded painfully in his chest. He wondered if Leila had meant what she said. Or was this all just a game? A distraction?

Suddenly the door was thrown open. A small, froglike woman peered outside. She had a scarf on her head and a broom in her hands.

"Hello?" she called out.

Leila clamped a hand over her mouth to stifle a laugh.

"Hello?"

The woman waited a moment longer before shutting the door.

"Did you see her?" said Leila, leaning back against the wall. "I knew it'd be a woman. You can tell by the garden."

"You're mad," said Mico, smiling in spite of himself. Leila's excitement was contagious.

"What now?" he said.

Leila threw him an impish glance.

"Now it's your turn."

"No way."

"All you've got to do is ring the bell."

"What if she catches us?"

Leila snorted.

"Like that's going to happen. Come on, Mico. You said you don't scare easy. Prove it."

Damn. Mico swore inwardly. Leila had him and she knew it. He couldn't back out now without looking like a coward. He stood up, his stomach jangling with nerves.

"Go on," said Leila, pushing him forward.

He walked slowly up the drive. He could almost feel the house glaring down at him, the windows watching like disapproving eyes. He forced himself to look ahead. Leila was right. He could do this.

He stopped outside the front door and glanced over his shoulder. Leila gave him a thumbs up. He nodded and turned back again. Taking a deep breath, he pressed the bell. To his astonishment, the door opened almost at once.

Mico blinked stupidly at the man in front of him. He was almost as big as Sy, but with an angry, red face and threatening eyes. He said something in French. Mico stared at him blankly.

"English?"

Mico nodded.

"What do you want?"

"I, er…" Mico felt the blood rush to his cheeks. All the words in his brain seemed to have evaporated. The man looked him up and down. Mico was suddenly aware of his scruffy appearance. At best, he probably looked like a tramp. At worst…

"From the camp?"

The question was more like an accusation.

"Yes."

There was no point denying it.

"What do you want?"

"I—"

Mico searched for an excuse. He failed spectacularly.

"You rang before, *non*?" said the man, his face twisting in sudden understanding. "Why? You looking to steal something, *non*?" He stepped forward and poked him in the chest.

"I know your type. Thieves, all of you."

Before Mico could reply, the man's hand clamped down on his arm.

"You picked the wrong house this time. I'm calling the police."

The words were like a switch in Mico's brain. Struggling violently, he tried to free himself but the man's grip was too strong.

"Get off!" he protested as the man slid a phone out of his pocket. "You're making a mistake. I'm not a thief."

"You have plenty of time to talk in the station. *Comprends?*"

Mico tugged harder, wishing he hadn't forgotten his knife in the tent. He wasn't sure what the police would do to him, but he didn't want to end up in jail. Who knew what might happen to him there? And where the hell was Leila? Was she still hiding? Or had she already made a run for it?

As if on cue, a loud ululating shout rang through the air. The man paused, the phone held to his ear. Mico almost cried out with relief. She hadn't left him.

There came another shout, shorter than the last. Then—

"Duck, Mico!" called Leila, popping out above the front wall.

Mico didn't need telling twice. As he dropped to his knees, a large stone came zipping through the air. It missed the man's head by millimetres and bounced off the front door. His face twisted in confusion.

"Eat rock, *y'kalb!*" roared Leila.

It was a glorious battle cry. The man's eyes widened as a barrage of hard pebbles came flying through the air towards him. He rattled something in French then let go of Mico and threw himself into the house.

Leila crowed triumphantly as Mico sprinted out the drive. Her hair flew in wild strands around her cheeks. A silver glint shone in her eyes. She looked, he thought, every bit the victorious general.

At that moment the front door was thrown open again. This time, the man was holding an air rifle. Leila's mouth dropped open.

84

"I teach you to come to my country," said the man.

"Pierre?"

The woman suddenly appeared in the doorway. It was obvious she hadn't seen them. Grabbing hold of the gun, she uttered something in French. It was all the distraction Mico needed. Before the man could recover, he grabbed hold of Leila and ran.

A shout rang out behind them. Mico flinched, expecting a bullet, but there was nothing. They ran out of the street, neither of them stopping until they'd put as much distance between them and the house as possible. When they could run no more, they threw themselves into an alley and lay there, panting.

Mico was the first to start laughing. He couldn't help it. It was as if all the tension inside him had broken free and bubbled to the surface. Once he'd started he couldn't stop.

"What a crazy man," said Leila next to him. Mico could tell she was annoyed about running away.

"I thought it was only America that let people keep guns."

"You're the crazy one," said Mico. "That's the most stupid thing I've ever done."

"I reckon we could still have taken him."

"He had a *gun*."

"Doesn't matter."

"You wouldn't be saying that if you'd got shot."

"We had these," said Leila, removing a handful of stones from her pocket. "Bet they would have done some damage."

"Oh, yeah," said Mico. "That's why he looked so scared."

She threw him a dirty look.

"Why'd you have them anyway?"

"There's loads around the camp. I carry them, in case."

Mico sat back on his elbows and regarded her with new respect.

"That's smart."

Leila tossed her hair at him.

"I am smart," she said.

But he could tell she was pleased.

14

A few days later, Mico and Leila were watching a group of new arrivals enter the camp. Now that the weather had improved more were turning up each week. Mico scowled as he saw the Lizard strolling past, the Crow shambling like a shadow behind him. It was obvious who was in charge.

"What we need," said Leila suddenly, "is a car." They were taking it in turns to pass an apple between them. "Aysha can't go on a truck because of the baby. And she can't jump a train."

Mico made a vague noise of assent. Leila followed his gaze to the Lizard.

"*Kalb*," she muttered.

"What?"

"It means dog."

"Say it again."

"*Kalb*."

Mico tried to copy her.

Leila giggled.

"Almost." She picked a bit of apple skin out of her

teeth. "Did you know Sara's been to see Judge Specs? She had a meeting with him yesterday."

Judge Specs was a hot-shot lawyer from Germany. He'd seen the camp on TV and come to offer his services free of charge. Everyone around the camp knew him. He operated underneath a tarp next to the library. Getting an appointment could take months but it was worth the wait. If Specs couldn't help you no-one could.

"I don't understand why you'd want to stay in France," continued Leila. Her nose crinkled in disgust. "They eat *snails*." She passed the apple to Mico. "Imagine if we had a car. We could drive to England ourselves."

Mico chewed thoughtfully.

"Back home, my uncle had a car. Bought it in the city. It wasn't new or anything. Yellow as chicken shit and covered in scratches. But it was his pride and joy. He wouldn't let me near it."

"What's your point?"

"A car's no good if you can't drive."

"Aysha can."

"On her own? All the way to England?"

"Why not?" said Leila.

"Sounds good. If you've got a car in your rucksack."

Leila's eyes narrowed.

"Don't be stupid, Mico," she said, handing him the apple core. She stood up and started walking away. "We're going to steal one."

Mico stared after her, unsure if she was joking.

"Is that your answer to everything?"

Leila didn't reply.

"Taking a car isn't like taking a bike," he said.

"I'm not forcing you to come," retorted Leila without turning around.

Mico swore. He should let her go alone. That would teach her a lesson. He drummed his fingers on his knees, watching as she walked off. He swore again.

"Wait up," he said, shoving the apple core into his mouth.

✭ ✭ ✭

"I've got cramp," whined Leila. She wriggled her foot, accidentally catching Mico on the shin.

"Watch it."

"Move over, then."

They were sitting on top of a low garden wall, their attention set on the house opposite. Their target was parked in the driveway.

"How long do you think he's going to be?" said Leila, wiggling her other foot.

He was the owner of the car, an elderly gentleman who they had been watching for five days. His routine was fixed. He took the car out once in the morning and once in the afternoon.

"What difference does it make? We have to wait anyway."

"Better to wait here than in the camp," said Leila, kicking her legs against the wall. "I hate it there. I hate that they call it the Jungle." She pointed to the houses. "We lived like that once. We went to school, went shopping, watched films. We didn't ask to leave our lives. Why can't they see? We're just like them. But we might as well be from another planet."

A shadow fell across her features as she spoke.

Suddenly she looked quite different; not like the Leila that Mico knew but a twisted reflection, a painting without colour.

Before he could reply there was movement opposite. "He's coming out."

The man got into the car and started the engine.

"We'll have to try again tom—" Mico stopped.

The man was going back into his house. More importantly, he'd left the car unlocked. Leila was already on her feet. The veil across her face had lifted and her eyes shone with excitement.

"Come on," she said, pulling him off the wall. "This is our chance. You remember the plan? We dump it as far away as we can. Then we go back for it when it's dark. By then, I'll have spoken to Aysha."

Mico stared at her.

"You mean you haven't asked her?"

Too late. Leila was already off. Mico shot after her. He got there first and threw himself into the front seat. Leila landed beside him a second later.

"Go on!" she said.

Mico glanced wildly at the controls.

"What do I do?"

"Press your foot on that," said Leila, pointing to a pedal.

"How do you know?"

"I've seen Aysha—"

She broke off. Mico followed her gaze to the front door. The old man was looking at them with his mouth open.

"Hit the pedal," cried Leila.

Mico did as he was told. At the same time, Leila crunched the gear stick into reverse.

"Now the accelerator. That one on the right. Hard as you can."

Mico pushed his foot down. With an almighty roar, the car sprang out into the road. Leila hooted in delight. Out of the corner of his eye, Mico saw the man shouting and waving his hands in the air. The sight of him filled Mico with sudden defiance. Twisting the steering wheel to the right, he jammed his foot on the accelerator. The car hurtled backwards in a wobbly line.

"Change gear," yelled Leila. "We're going the wrong way."

Mico wasn't listening. The car throbbed beneath his fingers. He could feel its power surging through him as if he was riding on the back of a fierce beast. He was unstoppable. He was invincible.

"Ya-waah," he whooped.

If only Uncle could see him now.

Just then the car flew across a dip in the road. Leila screamed. The steering wheel twisted violently in Mico's hand as they swerved towards a lamp post.

"We're going to hit it. Slow down."

A painful screeching sounded through the air as Mico slammed his foot on the brakes. The car jerked violently, snapping them in their seats.

"Shit," he said. His breath shook in heavy gasps.

Beside him, Leila moaned softly.

"Ow."

She touched her neck.

"That hurt."

Whether it was the adrenaline or the sheer failure of their plan, Mico couldn't help grinning. But his euphoria was abruptly broken by the unmistakeable sound of a siren. He swore.

91

"Leila? He's called the police. We need to go."

She didn't move.

"Wait, I'll come round."

With some difficulty, Mico slid out of the car. A thin hiss of air trailed from the tyres. As he opened Leila's door he heard a shout behind him. He turned around. The old man was heading in their direction. He caught Mico's eye and let out a quick volley of French. Without thinking, Mico drew out his knife and brandished it in the air.

"Stop," he cried.

The man wavered but carried on walking.

"I'll cut you," snarled Mico. As if to prove his intent he slashed the knife across the air. It didn't feel right to threaten an old man, but he couldn't let him come any closer. The man stopped. He was close enough now for Mico to see his face, not angry at all, but perplexed. Full of questions.

A pang of guilt flickered through him.

"Sorry," he muttered.

Then, knife in hand, he took hold of Leila and dragged her away.

15

Leila did not come to see Mico the following morning. Or the morning after that. On the third day, even Hassan was curious.

"What's the matter?" he asked. "You and your girlfriend had a fight?"

"She's not my girlfriend," growled Mico.

"Course she isn't."

Hassan grinned, clearly in a good mood. Over the past few days some of the friction seemed to have dissolved between him and Sy. They weren't talking properly yet, but they weren't ignoring each other either.

"You want to tell me about it?"

"Shove off, Hassan."

At that moment a savage cheer rose up outside. Mico and Hassan looked at each other. There was only one thing in the camp that sounded as loud and terrible as that.

"Where are you going?" asked Hassan as Mico stood up.

"I want to see what's happening."

Hassan frowned.

"If it's a fight you should stay away. You know how quickly they get out of control—"

Mico cut him off impatiently.

"You coming or not?"

They followed the noise to Omar's tent where a large crowd had gathered. Omar himself was sitting on a cloth on the ground with a spread of coins laid out in front of him. Men batted around him like fireflies. Mico saw their hands moving, flashes of silver, precious money exchanging palms with lightning speed. He heard Hassan's sharp breath. A second later, he saw him. Sy. Standing in the centre of the commotion, his chest bare, mouth pulled back.

"I'll take two of you," he roared. "Double money."

At once there was a great clamouring. More silver passed into Omar's hands, his nose twitching like a train on the tracks.

"He's fighting for *money*?" asked Mico. Hassan didn't answer. His face had gone pale. He looked like he was about to be sick.

The fight began. Two men, brothers perhaps, had taken up Sy's challenge. They circled him in slow motion, fists raised. Mico watched with a rising sense of disgust. There were no differences to settle here. This was all about fast cash. He wondered who'd thought of the idea. Omar, probably. He'd been stuck in the clinic for two weeks with nothing to do; no wonder he'd cooked up such a stupid scheme.

Suddenly one of the men lunged forward. Sy dodged him with ease. Swinging his right hand across the air he brought his fist down hard on the man's cheek. Mico heard a sickening crunch. The crowd drew a collective breath as he fell to the floor. Hassan swore. Sy swivelled round to meet his next opponent who took a wary step back.

"Come on," taunted Sy, his face glowing with sweat and adrenaline. Mico had never seen him like this before. It was almost as if he was *enjoying* it.

"This is madness," muttered Hassan. "He's going to get himself killed."

Mico didn't get a chance to ask who he meant.

With a bellow of desperation, the second challenger leapt towards Sy. He moved with surprising agility, darting clear of Sy's hands and landing a punch to his stomach. Sy doubled up with a low groan. His opponent, clearly sensing a win, came at him again. But he was overconfident. As he drew closer, Sy lashed out with his left hand, catching a blow to his ribs. The man reared backwards. Taking advantage of his hesitation, Sy charged forward and grabbed hold of his waist. Like an eel, the man wriggled free from his grasp. Before Sy could react he brought up his hand and smashed it into his chin.

Hassan swore again as Sy staggered backwards. Before Mico knew what was happening he was striding into the centre of the fight. It was like seeing a bird enter a circle of wolves. Only somehow Hassan looked fiercer and more dangerous than all the other men put together.

"You should be ashamed of yourselves," he shouted, positioning himself firmly between Sy and his opponent. "All of you. Is this why you're here? To gamble on each other's lives? The newspapers call this place the Jungle and they're right. You've travelled this far to find a better life for yourselves. But you're behaving like animals."

The men fell silent and looked down at their feet, the spell cast by the fight irreversibly broken. They stood there a moment as if uncertain what to do next. Then one by one they started to disperse.

Sy started to call them back, but it was no use. The fight was over. Out of the corner of his eye, Mico saw Omar hurriedly rolling their takings into a little pouch.

Hassan knelt down by the man on the ground. He hadn't moved since being hit.

"We better get him to the clinic," said Hassan, motioning Mico nearer.

"I'll help." Sy's opponent came forward. "He's my cousin."

As they struggled to get him upright, Sy moved to join them.

"No," said Hassan sharply. "You've done enough already."

✶ ✶ ✶

Later, Mico went to see Leila. He didn't want to spend the afternoon in his tent. He'd seen the look on Hassan's face when they'd returned from the clinic. He figured it was best to keep out of his way until he cooled down. In truth he didn't understand why Hassan was so angry. They both knew how desperate Sy was to earn money. Of course, they all wanted to leave the camp, but surviving day-to-day was hard enough. Sy was just playing the bigger game.

It wasn't until he was in sight of Leila's tent that

Mico remembered her sister. He'd seen her only once, at the football match. Thinking about her made him suddenly nervous. Would Leila have told her about the car? Is that why she hadn't come to see him? He hesitated. Perhaps he should go back. But he had come this far now. In any case it had been Leila's idea. Her sister couldn't blame him for that.

He stopped outside their tent.

"Leila?" he called.

There was no answer. He tried again, louder this time. There was a muffled grunt from inside.

"It's Mico. Can I come in?"

Another grunt.

Mico took this to mean yes. As he entered, he was struck by the strangest smell. His tent stank of sweat and unwashed clothes, but here it smelled sweet. It was pleasant but disorientating; like he'd stepped into a house and found himself in a garden instead. Then he saw why. Dozens of flowers were scattered along the borders of the tent. Pinks and purples and yellows cascading over each other in a patchwork of colour.

"Aysha's idea," said Leila, watching him. She was sitting cross-legged in a corner of the tent with a cushion wedged under her neck and her sketchbook on her lap.

"She's gone to collect some more. I don't see the point. They die so quickly. But she says it helps balance the stink outside."

"Does it?"

"You tell me."

"Smells better than mine," said Mico.

Leila gave him a withering look.

"That's because you're a boy." She closed her sketch-book and slid it into her rucksack. "What took you so long? I've been dying of boredom in here. Aysha had a fit when I told her what happened. She said I had to rest for a week."

"No more stealing cars, then?"

"You were the one who kept it in reverse," she said, folding her arms across her chest. "We'd have been fine if I'd been driving."

"We could try again."

"Forget it. Aysha said we wouldn't have made it. Not without the right contacts. Too many checkpoints."

She paused, her expression unexpectedly fierce.

"You never said you had a knife."

Mico shrugged.

"Does it matter?"

"You should have told me. We're supposed to be friends."

"I only carry it with me for protection."

"Is that why you were hiding it?"

"I wasn't hiding it. I forgot to tell you, all right?"

Leila looked unconvinced.

"You shouldn't have threatened the old man."

"I wasn't going to use it," said Mico, trying not to lose his temper. "I was just scaring him."

"That doesn't make it right."

"It wasn't right to steal his car either."

"That was different."

"How?"

"Because—"

Leila pursed her lips, her expression set into a stubborn frown. Unable to think of a convincing argument, she shrugged.

"If I were you I'd keep it in your tent. Next time, it could get us in serious trouble."

She reached in her pocket, drew out a handful of stones and held them out to him.

"If you have to, you can use these."

"What are they going to do?"

"You want them or not?"

She smirked triumphantly as Mico took them from her. Then she sucked in a deep breath through her teeth. "I'm going crazy in here. What's happening outside?"

Mico thought back to the fight.

"Nothing," he said.

"Nothing?"

"I didn't see the Doctor when I walked past his tent."

"That's it?"

"Well, he's always sitting outside," said Mico defensively.

Leila made a face. It was the same face his uncle would make when he found out a chicken had escaped from the farm.

Mico drew an impatient breath.

"All right. A giant hole's opened up in the middle of the camp. There are reporters everywhere and they're paying a load of money to anyone who knows how it got there."

Leila's mouth twitched but she kept a straight face.

"You'll have to do better than that."

Mico thought for a moment.

"And a circus truck broke down outside the camp. Someone opened one of the cages and accidentally let out a lion. The Ghost-Men got eaten."

"Both of them?"

"Yeah," said Mico, warming to his story. "But the lion

was still hungry so it ate the reporters too. Then it went to the port and drank all the water from the sea. Every last drop. Then it lay itself down like a gold carpet and grew bigger and bigger until its head was on one shore and its tail on the other. People are already walking across."

"That is the dumbest thing I've ever heard," said Leila, but she laughed anyway. They were still conjuring wild tales when Aysha entered the tent.

"I found some more purple ones," she began, holding up a bunch of flowers. Her eyes fell on Mico.

"Oh—"

"This is Mico," said Leila. Then, by way of explanation, "He's not as stupid as he looks."

Mico glared at her.

"You'll have to forgive my sister," said Aysha, dropping the flowers at the side of the tent. "She was born wild. I've been trying to tame her ever since."

Leila nodded at Aysha's stomach.

"How's baby?" she asked.

"Sleeping," replied Aysha, levering herself carefully to the ground. "I don't think it likes it here anymore than we do."

"*She*," said Leila with emphasis. "It's going to be a girl."

Aysha smiled. Her eyes were pale green and round like almonds. She was bigger than when she'd first arrived in camp; her dress clung tightly onto her arms, outlining the hard contours of her muscles. It struck Mico that the two sisters could not have been more different. Leila fizzed and sparked like a firecracker but Aysha was as solid as a bear.

"So you were the one who helped my sister steal a car?" she said mildly.

Mico flushed.

"Leave him alone, Aysh," said Leila. "I've told you already. It was my idea."

"I'm sure it was. That's why, from next week, I want you to report back to me every hour."

"Why?"

"I need to know you're not in trouble."

"But I don't even have a watch."

"Then you better be careful you're not late."

Leila spat out a word that Mico didn't understand. Her face smouldered with outrage.

"Language, Leila. You'll be responsible for making sure she's on time," Aysha continued, looking at Mico. He opened his mouth to protest but the expression on her face was so stern that he shut it again at once. In the background, Leila was huffing and puffing to outmatch a chimney. Her sister took no notice.

"Sara mentioned that you are a sensible boy. Leila does not always appreciate that her actions can have consequences. I hope I can trust you not to try anything like that again?"

Mico nodded.

Leila threw him a foul look.

"I was only trying to get out of here," she muttered. "This place eats people."

Aysha snorted.

"It's true. They come in but not everyone makes it out."

Aysha drew a pair of knitting needles and a ball of yarn out of her bag.

"You know we had no choice," she said quietly. "It wasn't safe for us there anymore."

A brief scowl passed across Leila's face and disappeared.

"Aysha's friend arranged for us to come to France," she said, turning to Mico. "Our uncle is already in England. That's why we want to start a new life there. After Jahir—"

She stopped and glanced at her sister as if worried she might have said something she shouldn't have.

"My husband was killed in riots," said Aysha without looking up. The needles clicked sharply in her hands. "The government had increased taxes. People were unhappy. Jahir was coming back from work. He never came home."

"I'm sorry," said Mico. He searched for something to add, but nothing seemed right. The needles snapped through the air like angry tongues. After a few minutes Mico could stand the silence no longer.

"We had a chicken farm," he began. He had never shared his story with anyone before, not even Hassan. Now the words tumbled over each other in his hurry to get them out. When he reached the part about Esther his voice broke.

"It's OK," whispered Leila, squeezing up beside him.

Having her there helped. Mico felt the tightness in his chest loosen a little, felt his breath grow a little steadier. It was as if, in that moment, they had all become bound by the same thread. Later, he would remember that feeling. The realisation that nothing joined humans so much as pain.

"It was brave of you to leave on your own," said Aysha at last.

"I did what I had to," said Mico.

"Then I wish there had been another way."

"That's a stupid thing to wish," said Leila. "You can't change the past." She paused. "Want to know what I wish for? *Basbousa*. Soaked in coconut syrup." Her eyes gleamed. "It's the best dessert you could ever eat."

"I wish for a proper bed," said Mico simply.

"A clean pair of socks," said Aysha.

"A new set of paints."

"Trainers."

"Chicken curry."

With each wish, Mico felt himself grow lighter. It was as if the air was soaking up their words, growing heavier each time one of them spoke. By the time evening fell it was almost electric. Clouds gathered on the horizon, flexing their muscles at the camp below.

But it wasn't until Mico stumbled back to his tent that the sky exploded. He did not run for cover. Instead he looked up and opened his mouth, arms outspread as wishes rained down upon him as cool and hard as gold coins.

16

On the fourth day of Leila's curfew a dead body was found on the beach. A young man in a baggy wetsuit.

"Fool tried to swim across," explained Sy. "What was he thinking? It's the Channel not a swimming pool."

By the time Mico and Leila went to see for themselves the police had removed the body and taped off a section of the beach. The port was crawling with reporters. They moved like hyenas, gnashing at the officers' heels for information.

It didn't take long before one set eyes on them.

"Afternoon," he said, blocking their path. "David Roe. I report for BN News." He flashed a card at them. "Terrible tragedy, this. I don't suppose you'd care for an interview?"

Mico glowered at him.

"I can pay," he continued, shaking a wallet at them. "Good money." He looked around then leant in conspiratorially.

"I'll throw in an extra fifty if you say you're family. How about that?"

Leila smiled sweetly.

"No English," she said.

"Not a problem, sweetheart. I brought my translator with me. If you'd just give me a moment."

As soon as he'd disappeared into the crowd, Mico and Leila took their chance and legged it.

"You didn't want the money?" asked Mico.

"Did you?" said Leila.

"No."

"Me neither."

And that was all either of them said about it.

The first thing they noticed when they got back to the camp was Hassan coming out of the Doctor's tent. He looked worried. In his hands was a bag filled with the Doctor's belongings.

"What's going on?" said Mico. "Where's the Doctor?"

"He's sick," said Hassan. "Sy's with him now."

Mico blinked in surprise. Until that morning, Hassan had been pretending Sy didn't exist. What had changed?

"They're at the clinic. It took them ages to get inside. You know what the queue's like. The Doctor asked me to bring him a few things."

Mico was suddenly struck by an unpleasant thought. If Hassan and Sy were talking again then the Doctor's condition must be a whole lot worse than Hassan was letting on.

"Is he going to be OK?" asked Leila.

Hassan hesitated a fraction longer than he should have. Without waiting for an answer, Mico grabbed Leila's arm and pulled her towards the clinic, all thoughts of getting her back to her sister forgotten.

Amid a flurry of outraged shouts, they sprinted past the queue of people waiting outside and hurled themselves into the tent. As usual it was heaving. A swarm of volunteer doctors and nurses buzzed around the patients. The air stank of disinfectant and sweat.

They hadn't gone more than a few paces when a nurse barred their way.

"You can't come in here," she said, folding her arms across her chest. "There's not enough space for visitors."

Mico opened his mouth to argue when Sy appeared in front of them. He whispered in the nurse's ear. Mico didn't catch what he said, but his words had an immediate effect.

"I'm sorry," said the nurse. She threw a pitying glance at Mico and Leila before hurrying past them.

"Self-righteous cow," hissed Leila under her breath.

"He's at the end," said Sy.

"Where are you going?" asked Mico as he turned away.

"Omar's. I'll be back later."

Mico did not bother to reply. He was cross at Sy for thinking about money when the Doctor was sick. Sensing his irritation, Leila touched him lightly on the arm.

As they walked past the beds, Mico tried not to look at the people around him. If the camp sometimes felt like a waiting room this place was a battlefield. A lot of the patients wore bandages. Others stared blankly into space. A couple of beds ahead a man was being sick into a bucket. Mico felt Leila squeeze his hand as they shuffled past. Her lips were pressed together as if she was trying not to cry.

The Doctor was sitting on a makeshift bed with a tube of fluid sticking out of his arm. His face was paler than Mico had ever seen it. He felt a sudden pang of guilt for not checking on him when he'd passed his tent the other day.

"Ah, Mico."

The Doctor's face lit up as he saw them. The skin around his eyes crinkled like paper.

"The boy with hair that curls like wire."

His eyes moved to Leila.

"And the fighter."

He coughed. It was a drum-rattle, hoarse and painful.

"A fine combination, yes. Strong. Not like me, yes. I'm an old man now, yes. This place – it's made me old. Hah!"

"You're going to get better," said Mico, trying to keep the uncertainty from his voice. "The government are going to take you home. Remember?"

The Doctor laughed and coughed again. Mico exchanged an anxious look with Leila.

"Some advice I give you, Baba. Don't lie to a dying man, yes. He might come after you, yes."

"You're not dying," said Mico fiercely. Razi's death was still raw in his memory. He couldn't bear another. "They'll take you to the hospital before they let anything happen to you. Tell him, Leila."

She nodded, unable to speak.

The Doctor shook his head.

"No hospital for me. I've told them."

"Why not?"

The Doctor patted Mico's hand. "I know this body, yes. It has been good to me. But now it's tired. It needs rest. Why punish it? I want to die with friends. Not in a hospital."

"But—"

107

"No buts, Mico." He yawned. "Now let me sleep, yes. Waiting in that queue made me tired."

A glimmer of alarm crossed Leila's face as he lay his head back against the pillow.

"Don't look like that, girl. I'm not dying yet."

17

Mico stayed with the Doctor through the afternoon. At some point he was aware of Leila speaking to him, but when he turned towards her she had disappeared. She returned some time later with flowers which she placed on top of the Doctor's blanket. Then she was gone again and it was Hassan who took her place. After Hassan, it was Sy. Once or twice they tried speaking to him, even Sy, but their words sounded distant as if they were talking through water. Eventually they gave up.

It was late by the time they were finally ushered out of the clinic. Mico started to protest, but the doctors were firm. Their patients needed rest. Mico hardly slept. The one time he did drop off he dreamt that the Ghost-Men were standing around the Doctor's bed. They stood there in silence waiting for him to wake up. When he did open his eyes, they took a pillow and laid it over his face.

That's when he woke up.

He was back at the clinic first thing in the morning. The Doctor looked worse than he had the day before.

A thin sheen of sweat glistened across his upper lip and his face was flushed. The drum-rattle in his chest was louder, more frequent. It struck Mico that this was what death sounded like – not mighty and victorious, but meek.

"You look better than yesterday," he lied.

"Like new, yes," said the Doctor. "How are you, Baba? Good, good, hm?"

"Same as I was yesterday. Same as I'll be tomorrow."

The Doctor chuckled and wheezed painfully. The sound clamped down on Mico's heart. The Doctor had been the first one to speak to him when he'd arrived. The Ghost-Men had left him at the port. He'd followed the rest of the shipment to the camp then wandered around for hours, carrying his pathetic sack of belongings with him, until the Doctor called him over. He must have seen how hungry Mico was because the first thing he did was offer him ginger nuts. They were about the only thing he ever seemed to eat. Mico couldn't imagine life in the camp without him.

"Do something for me, Mico," said the Doctor. He pointed to the tiny pile of belongings at the foot of his bed.

"My shoes, give them to me."

"Why?"

"I am getting ready, yes."

Mico did not dare ask what for. The Doctor hugged the shoes close to his chest like a talisman and smiled.

"Now my scarf. Put it on my neck, yes. If I die here, God will know where to put me in my next life, hm?"

He sighed in happiness as Mico draped the cloth across his neck.

"Red Devils forever," he said, raising a weak hand.

Then he coughed so hard it was as if the skin was being grated from the inside of his chest.

"Tell me about Crawley," said Mico in desperation. "Tell me about your shop."

The Doctor smiled weakly.

"Ah, my shop, yes. But you hear that story many times, hm? Today I tell you another." He coughed again. Mico handed him a bowl to spit in and waited. It was another few minutes before the Doctor could begin.

"My father was a smith, yes. All day he pound that metal. You can smell the fire on him when he come home. Always he smell like that. Burnt. I apprentice to him when I am fifteen. But it is hard work, hm. When I am twenty I pack a bag and run away. Over the sea, yes, to England."

He paused. When he spoke again his voice was wistful.

"It would be good to see it again, yes."

"England?"

"The sea. I ask already, but the doctors, yes, they say no. They say I am too weak. Hah!"

Mico did not reply, but his mind was already churning. When Leila arrived that afternoon, he told her what he was thinking.

"But we can't just get him out of here unnoticed," she hissed.

The Doctor stirred in his sleep.

"Someone will stop us," she continued in a low whisper.

"That's why we need a distraction."

"Like what?"

Mico bit his lip and glanced around the tent. At that

moment, Hassan walked in. He smiled.

"I think I know what to do."

They put their plan into action later that evening. Leila had got special permission from Aysha to stay out past her hourly curfew. Hassan and Sy were with the Doctor. Admittedly, Sy had taken a bit of convincing, but when Mico had told him he was going to do it with or without his help, he'd finally agreed. Besides he owed the Doctor; he was the one who'd introduced him to Omar.

As decided, Mico was waiting in the queue outside the clinic. He had no intention of going in. His job was to bring everyone *out*.

He stiffened as he saw a flash of yellow drawing towards him. It was time to begin.

"Hey," he said as Leila pushed into the queue past him. "I was here first."

Leila didn't even bother turning around. Mico nudged her impatiently.

"I'm talking to you."

"Don't touch me," she retorted, glaring at him.

"You started it. There's a queue here in case you didn't notice. Get in line."

"Or what?"

Mico nudged her again, harder this time.

"Or I'll make you."

Leila snorted.

"What you going to do, monkey boy?"

"What did you call me?"

"You heard."

By now, the two of them had the attention of the entire queue. Mico stepped forward.

"Say that again."

112

"Say what, monkey boy," said Leila mockingly.

Mico gave her a gentle shove.

"I'm telling you. Get to the back."

Leila pushed him back.

"And I told you. Don't touch me."

They eyed each other up for a moment. Then Leila winked at him.

"Monkey boy," she said loudly.

With a strangled cry, Mico threw himself forwards and grabbed hold of her hair. Leila twisted away from him and aimed a kick at his legs. She missed. Mico hurled a fist at her face, hit air instead. Voices rose up around them as they wrestled each other to the ground.

"What's going on here? Stop it, I say! Stop it!"

"Let go of me," yelled Mico, as two strong arms lifted him away from Leila. He swung himself round with his fists raised into the air.

"Easy now," said the curly-haired man opposite him. The tag on his chest read *Dr Costello*.

"Relax, kid. You want to explain what's going on here?"

Mico's eyes flickered to the clinic where other staff had emerged, curious to see what the noise was about. He had no way of knowing how many were still inside.

Dr Costello was watching him expectantly. Mico pointed to Leila.

"She jumped the line."

"He's lying," said Leila, sitting up.

"Ask anyone."

Dr Costello took a deep breath.

"Look, I know it's tough out here but there's no reason to behave like this. Don't you think we've got enough to worry about without you hurting each other?"

He spoke calmly but Mico could detect the frustration behind his words.

"I know you're tired. You've been waiting a long time. But we're doing all we can with the resources we have." He put a hand on Mico's shoulder.

"No more fighting, understand? You're just slowing us down."

Mico watched in alarm as Dr Costello turned back to the clinic. The others were also starting to go inside. But it was too soon. The same thought must have occurred to Leila, for almost at once she began to wail.

"He's going to kill me."

Dr Costello hesitated before turning back towards her. Leila's face was the picture of innocence. If she failed as an artist, Mico thought, she'd make a fine performer.

"Don't leave me here. He's evil. I've seen it in his eyes."

"I've spoken to him," said Dr Costello, bending down beside her. "Nothing's going to happen to you."

"Please stay," said Leila, throwing her arms around his neck. "I'll be safe with you."

Mico bit back a smile as Dr Costello struggled to free himself from her grip. She wasn't making it easy for him.

Suddenly a cry broke free of the clinic. Two nurses ran out, shouting over each other. With some difficulty, Dr Costello managed to tug himself away from Leila and stand up.

"What is it?" he growled.

"He's gone."

Mico's heart skipped a beat.

"What are you talking about? Who's gone?"

North York Central Library 416-395-5535

Toronto Public Library

User ID: 2 ********** 6130

Date Format: DD/MM/YYYY

Number of Items: 2

Item ID:37131193255445
 Title:The jungle
 Date due:20/03/2019

Item ID:37131193260809
 Title:Star by star
 Date due:20/03/2019

Telephone Renewal# 416-395-5505
www.torontopubliclibrary.ca
Wednesday, February 27,   3:10 PM
2019

"Farid Musa."

For a moment Mico was confused. He glanced at Leila who glowered at him meaningfully. Then it hit him. Farid must be the Doctor's real name. Funny how he had never thought to ask.

Dr Costello was still having difficulty understanding.

"The pneumonia patient? That's impossible. He was too weak to stand."

The nurses answered simultaneously.

"He's not there."

"Wanted to go to the sea."

"Didn't listen."

"Should have kept an eye on him."

A ruffle of murmurs started up in the queue. This was the most excitement any of them had seen for a long time.

"He can't have gone," said Doctor Costello again. "Not on his own anyway. He would have needed help."

As he spoke his eyes fell on the girl on the ground. She was watching him closely. Doctor Costello's face crumpled in thought. He glanced at the boy who was watching him with equal intensity. As a father of three children himself, Dr Costello knew when he'd been had. His mouth twitched. Mico braced himself, ready to run. But Dr Costello merely threw his hands into the air and turned to the queue.

"I can't do anything about a missing patient. But it appears we have an empty bed. Who's next?"

18

Sy and Hassan were waiting for them outside the camp. They had bundled the Doctor into a blanket. Sy was carrying him in his arms. Mico swallowed. The Doctor's eyes were closed but he could hear the low rasp of his breath as he dozed. He looked so frail and thin. Like a baby.

"You made it."

Hassan swung a fist at Mico's shoulder.

"Good job."

Sy rolled his eyes.

"Let's move. It's getting late."

The streets were quiet. The interest surrounding the dead man seemed to have disappeared and there wasn't a single reporter in sight. On the beach the police tape had been tugged loose. It fluttered in the breeze like a leftover party streamer.

"They didn't waste time packing up," muttered Sy. The bitterness in his voice was unmistakeable. Hassan said something Mico couldn't make out, but Sy merely grunted and trudged on ahead.

The sea that night looked darker than Mico had ever seen it. If he listened carefully he could hear it whispering. The ripples and swells hummed across the air like a song. If he scrunched his eyes up tight he could see other colours dancing in the water – purples and whites and greens as if there was a whole other world shifting under its surface.

The Doctor stirred as Sy rested him gently on the sand. He drew a sharp breath as he caught sight of the water.

"So beautiful. Like a woman, yes. A goddess. Hah!"

He laid aside the shoes still clutched in his arms.

"I must make an offering." He motioned Mico towards him. "Put them in the water, Baba." Sy's face contorted in disbelief but he kept his mouth shut. Mico went forward and placed the shoes, still wrapped in newspaper, by the water's edge. They floated out a little way before sinking without a sound.

Leila moved up beside him to watch.

"Can you feel them?" she whispered in his ear. "The ghosts?"

Mico thought back to another night, another encounter, another pair of shoes in the deep.

"There's no such thing as ghosts," he said.

"If I was younger," said the Doctor, "younger and stronger, yes, I would chance it." He pointed a bony finger. "I would swim the Channel back to England, hm."

For a moment, no-one said anything. They all knew that what he was suggesting was impossible. The dead man had proved it. But the Doctor didn't know about him yet and none of them wanted to be the first to tell him.

117

"You would die before you got there," said Sy eventually.

"You don't know that, yes."

Sy shook his head. When he spoke his voice was firm. "It would be a worthless journey."

"Hah!" said the Doctor. He paused for a moment, staring out at the horizon. "There is no such thing."

They stayed there a while looking out across the sea, listening to the endless whispers of the waves. Then the Doctor began shivering and it was time to take him back. He died three days later. Unlike Razi's death, the Doctor's passing was a quiet affair. He simply slipped out of existence like a ripple across water. Later, when Mico passed his tent he saw there was already another man in his place. If there was anything good that came out of his death, it was that Hassan and Sy were back on speaking terms. But that wasn't enough for Mico.

"I should have done something," he said to Leila.

"But you couldn't have," she said one evening when he brought up the subject again. It was only the two of them in her tent. Aysha had gone to congratulate Sara. Thanks to Judge Specs her asylum claim had been accepted. She was leaving the camp in the morning. The timing could not have been more fortunate. The evening before the Ghost-Men had left to intercept a shipment coming from Greece. Sara would be gone before the Lizard returned. Mico had already said his goodbyes. It had been hard trying to feel happy for her when, in truth, he felt nothing but an overwhelming sense of hopelessness.

"The doctors should have helped him," he said.

"They tried."

"They should have tried harder."

Leila blinked, taken aback by the anger in his voice.

"The Doctor always thought the government would send him home. He was an old man, Leila. He didn't deserve to die in this place. No-one does."

"I never said he did."

"My uncle wanted a better life for me. He thought I'd find it if I left. But he was wrong. This place – they think we're animals. They don't care." He looked down at his hand and raised it in the air. "Maybe if we didn't look like this. Maybe they'd help us then."

"You're being stupid."

"What about you?" Mico hit back, more furious than he'd ever been. "Weren't you being stupid when you tried to steal a car?"

"Shut up," said Leila hotly.

"Have you ever thought about your sister? What happens when the baby comes? Have you thought about that?"

"Shut up, Mico."

"Are you going to bring it up in this shithole? Is that what you want?"

"SHUT UP. SHUT UP. SHUT UP."

Leila's voice rose even higher than Mico's. Her face had gone red, her fists clenched by her sides. She looked ready to punch him and suddenly Mico didn't know whether to feel angry or ashamed. Just then there came another cry from outside. Then a second, louder than the first. The sound was too pitiful to ignore.

With a poisonous glare in his direction, Leila stood up and followed the noise out of the tent. Mico waited a beat before going after her. A small knot of people had gathered outside. They stood in a circle, surrounding the pair of boys fighting in the dirt. One had straddled the other and was punching him as if his life depended on it. He paused momentarily to clear the tangle of hair from his eyes; only then did Mico recognise him.

"Tamal! Stop it!"

The crowd parted as Sara came running out of her tent. Mico saw Aysha lumbering a little way behind her.

"Take it back!"

"Tamal, what are you doing?"

Sara grabbed him round the waist and lifted him into the air.

"Let go of me. He deserves it, *Ami*."

"Calm down, Tamal."

Sara swung him round and placed him on the ground with her arms fixed firmly on his shoulders. The crowd shifted a little, unsure if they should stay.

"Why are you fighting?" asked Sara, bending down so that her face was level with his.

"He said *Abba*'s dead."

Tamal's eyes were wet and a nasty bruise was starting to spread across his cheek. His opponent looked far worse.

"He called you a liar. He said *Abba*'s not coming, but that's not true. *Abba*'s alive. He's going to meet us tomorrow in the new place."

"Oh, Tamal."

Sara's voice broke a little as she spoke and for the first time Mico saw a wave of doubt cross Tamal's face.

"He *is* coming, isn't he?"

Sara did not reply. Perhaps, thought Mico, she had run out of lies.

120

"I was going to tell you."

"No."

Tamal pulled away from her like he'd been stung. He shook his head.

"You're lying," he shouted. "*Abba*'s alive. And if you won't find him I will."

Before anyone could stop him, he turned and fled through the crowd.

"Come back, Tamal."

Sara started to follow him, but she was shaking too much to stand and after a few steps she collapsed onto the ground. A murmur rose up in the circle around her. As one the crowd slipped away. They recognised despair when they saw it and they knew it was catching.

Aysha was the only one to come forward. She lowered herself to the ground and wrapped her arms around Sara. Her eyes searched the dispersing circle until they locked on Leila and Mico.

"Find him," she mouthed.

Leila was off at once.

"Wait," hollered Mico, running after her. "She asked both of us."

"Hurry up then," Leila yelled over her shoulder.

"Where are we going?"

"To the entrance."

"How do you know that's where he is?"

"Because I do. Now hurry up!"

When they got to the front of the camp it was empty.

"He's not here," said Mico, drawing to a halt. He bent down to catch his breath. "What now?"

"But there's no other way out," murmured Leila. "Unless he's already left."

The two of them looked at each other. Without a word

121

they sprinted out into the main road. Leila exhaled in relief. Tamal was sitting a little way down on the pavement. As they drew nearer he wiped his eyes fiercely.

"Go away," he growled.

Mico hung back but Leila dumped herself down beside him as if she hadn't heard.

"Why'd you run?" she asked.

Silence.

"You know both my parents—"

"He's not dead," interrupted Tamal. "Don't even think about saying different or I'll hit you."

Leila raised her eyebrows. Then she slid her sketchbook out of her rucksack.

"Want to see something cool?"

Silence.

Humming to herself, Leila flicked through the pages. Mico had never seen inside her sketchbook before. He leant his head across, curious, but Leila was going too fast for him to get a decent look. She stopped suddenly and pushed the book onto Tamal's lap.

"What do you see?"

Mico squinted at the picture she had chosen. It didn't look like much – just a bunch of coloured squiggles, lines and shapes. It certainly didn't look like art. But as he looked closer, the squiggles and lines began changing in front of his eyes, shifting and merging until, out of the muddle in front of him, he saw it. A woman's face.

He whistled softly.

"I don't see nothing," said Tamal, screwing his face up to the paper.

Leila smiled and held the page at arm's length in the air.

"How about now?"

"I still don't—"

Tamal stopped and blinked. He rubbed his eyes and looked again.

"It's a trick," he whispered.

"No, not a trick. An illusion."

"A what?"

Leila paused, trying to find the right way to explain.

"Sometimes when we look at something we don't really see it the way we should. Sometimes, to understand, we have to look a second time."

Tamal thought for a moment. Then he scowled.

"When people look at me they see a little boy," he said. "But I'm not little." He clenched his fists. "I'm almost eleven."

Mico swallowed. It was exactly the sort of thing Esther would have said.

"Eleven?" Leila pretended to look impressed. "Almost a man. But men don't run away when they get frightened about something. I mean, brave men don't."

"I'm not frightened," said Tamal. He sniffed. "And I'm not running anywhere."

As they walked back through the camp later, Mico apologised.

"I didn't mean to shout like that," he said, as Tamal ran off ahead of them. "Some of the things I said—" He faltered, embarrassed. "I'm sorry."

Leila nodded, but did not reply. They continued, side by side, the space between them itching with the prickly silence of remembered words. At last, Mico could stand it no longer.

"That thing you showed Tamal – the illusion – where did you learn to draw something like that?" he asked.

For a minute, Leila didn't say anything. There was a faraway expression in her eyes as if she was back in another place, another time. Her face was twisted with pain. It struck Mico then that the reason she behaved so tough all the time was because she was hurting inside. She was just too proud to let anyone see. He realised he knew little about her past, about who she might have been outside the camp.

"Leila?" he said softly.

She replied without looking at him.

"Jahir taught me. Aysha's husband." She sighed, suddenly relenting. "Our parents died when I was small. Aysha was already working as a journalist by then. She looked after me. I was too young to understand why but the government never liked what she wrote. She showed a side of the country they didn't want people to see. But she was always careful. For me.

"When she met Jahir I was worried I wouldn't like him. But he was a good man. Kind. After he died, Aysha changed. She started to attack the government directly." Leila paused. "I guess she went too far. One night, they sent the police to arrest her. Accused her of selling state secrets. We only just got away."

They were almost at the tent. Tamal turned and grinned, his bruise flashing like a light bulb. They slowed, watching in silence as he threw himself inside. Even from where they were standing, Sara's delight was audible.

"Do you ever think about going back?" asked Mico.

"All the time," said Leila. "But then I think what they would do to Aysha if they caught her." She looked up at the darkening sky. The air was turning cold. A few

124

stray birds looped across, chasing the last of the day to their nests.

"There was a story Jahir used to tell me. About how the first humans were born with wings. Can you imagine what that would be like? To fly anywhere in the world without worrying about having the right papers?"

Mico looked at her. In his mind he saw a pair of silvery wings on Leila's back, saw her lift into the air and soar towards the horizon. Then he saw himself standing alone on the ground, a dot growing smaller and smaller.

"It's just a story," he said.

"Yeah." Leila shivered and wrapped her arms around her chest. "That's what I used to tell him."

19

Mico stooped down to pick another bunch of flowers.

"You can stop now," said Leila. She was smiling but her eyes were sad. Since Sara's departure, she had been quieter, more thoughtful. Once or twice, Mico had caught her looking up at the sky. Watching the birds. As if they could teach her how to spread out her arms and fly.

"We've got enough."

"These aren't for your tent," said Mico. "They're for mine."

The two of them were exploring the woods behind the camp. Aysha had sent them to collect flowers. They should have started heading back a while ago, but neither was in a hurry to get back.

"Do you think the Doctor might have been right?" Leila asked.

"About what?" said Mico, lingering a little way behind her. A clump of lilac flowers had caught his eye and he was calculating if he could jump the fierce thorn bush in front of them. It didn't look too hard, he decided, stepping back to give himself enough momentum.

"Do you think you could swim to England? I know that man died, but maybe he wasn't a strong swimmer. It might still be possible. Mico? Are you listening?"

Leila turned to find Mico standing, immobile, his eyes fixed on something in the undergrowth.

"What is it?" she said, moving back towards him. "What have you found? Is it a snake? Ow!"

She had already stepped into the bush before suddenly, painfully, realising it was full of thorns.

"Damn it, Mico. You could have told me."

Still cursing, she walked back a little way, then ran at full pelt, crossing the bush in a single bound.

"You wouldn't have to swim," murmured Mico as she landed beside him. "Not if you had one of these."

It was then that Leila saw it. She blinked, unable to believe her eyes.

It was a boat.

"Impossible," she breathed, moving past Mico to get a closer look. "How did it get here?"

Behind the thorn bush there was a slight hollow in the ground and it was here that the boat was resting. It was covered in leaves and stray branches. They were scattered across it like a glorious, glossy hide. It was old, too. Its sides were lined with dirt and there were faint cracks in the body where the wood had started to age and rot.

As Leila scrambled down into the hollow, Mico had a sudden urge to call out a warning. The boat didn't seem man-made at all. It was like a wild flower that had taken root and grown from the earth itself. What if it was a trick? A trap left there by the tree-spirits that Esther had told him about?

127

"Maybe we should leave it," he said.

Leila looked at him as if he were crazy.

"It's just a bit of dirt, Mico," she replied, mistaking the fear in his voice. "Come on. Help me get these leaves out. I want to see how big it is."

Hesitating slightly, Mico slid down into the hollow beside her. Leila was working like someone possessed, throwing out handfuls of leaves until her hands and face were smudged in heavy streaks of dirt. But no tree-spirits came to protest; the boat didn't disappear.

"It's real," said Mico, touching the wood with his hand. He couldn't believe it. But as Leila cleared the last of the foliage, his heart dropped. In the centre of the boat was a hole.

"There's a paddle," said Leila, her voice rising in excitement. She held up two halves of an oar.

"It's broken."

"We can fix it."

"How?"

Leila wasn't listening.

"It's smaller than I thought," she said, surveying the boat with her head tilted to one side. "Could hold three people just about. Guess someone must have dumped it here."

"Doesn't matter. See that hole. It'll sink in no time."

Leila flexed the two oar fragments on either shoulder, a slow smile spreading across her face.

"Look, wings."

The gesture filled Mico with sudden irritation.

"We can't fix it," he said again, unable to stop an edge of frustration creeping into his voice. "We've got no tools, no money. We wouldn't even know where to start."

Leila straightened up.

128

"Listen to yourself," she said. "Can't you see? We've found a boat, Mico. This is our chance. We don't have to stay here anymore. We can leave." She put the oars down. Her voice dropped slightly, trembling with the strength of her conviction.

"Maybe you're right. Maybe we won't be able to fix it. But that doesn't mean we can't try."

Her eyes burnt into his in silent challenge. Mico could feel her peering deep into him, into his soul, measuring his worth. Just like Esther when she'd set him a dare. Only this time he had nothing left to lose.

He bent down, picked up a stone and scratched a line against the surface of the wood. He held the stone out to Leila who regarded him with bemusement.

"We have to make it ours," he said.

Leila's mouth curled into a smile as she understood his meaning. She knelt down beside him and carved another line next to his own. Her tongue stuck out in concentration as she worked. As if, Mico thought, she was sculpting a work of art.

"There," she said, sitting back. "What do you think?"

The line he had drawn had been transformed into a bird. Mico traced its shape with his finger, slowly tracking the contours of its wings. He squeezed Leila's hand.

"It's perfect."

✶ ✶ ✶

When they got back to the camp later that afternoon Aysha was already waiting for them.

"You're late," she said, casting a suspicious eye over their clothes. "Where have you been?"

Leila looked offended.

"I thought you'd lifted the curfew."

Aysha folded her arms expectantly.

"We were getting the flowers," said Leila with a dramatic sigh. "*You* asked us to, remember?"

Mico looked down at his trainers. Leila had already sworn him to secrecy about the boat. But Aysha had eyes like lasers. Given the chance she'd pluck out the truth without him uttering a single word.

"I asked you to pick the flowers not crawl through them. Why are you so dirty?"

"I don't know. Maybe because we had to walk through *grass* and *mud*."

"Very funny," said Aysha. She handed Leila a rag. "Here. You can clean the tent."

"Why?"

"You've just brought in all that *grass* and *mud* with you."

She glanced at Mico.

"You can help too if you're staying."

"Actually, I was going," he said, backing away.

"I'll come over when I'm done," said Leila, throwing him a meaningful look.

"Who said you're going to be allowed?" said Aysha.

Mico could still hear them arguing as he went. They had left the boat almost exactly as they'd found it. As an extra precaution Leila had covered it with more leaves in case anyone happened to pass by. Mico had been keen to move it somewhere else, but Leila had pointed out that nobody had found it until now so it was probably as safe there as it was anywhere. Besides, she said, as they returned to the camp, no-one would be stupid enough to poke around a thorn bush, not even if they were caught short.

He hadn't gone more than a few metres when he spotted the Lizard emerging from Sara's tent. He didn't look happy. Mico slowed. He knew he should ignore him and carry on but for some reason he couldn't.

"She's gone," he said, doing nothing to hide the smile on his face. "They left this morning."

The Lizard's eyes thinned.

"Mico, yes?" He stopped opposite him, so close that Mico could smell his breath, rotten as hell.

"Why you so happy, boy? You leaving too?"

Mico's momentary glee popped and deflated like a balloon. The Lizard saw and took a step closer, the sharp metal of his belt pressing into Mico's stomach.

"Remember one thing. You want to stay in France that your choice. But you want to cross the Channel, you need my help."

Mico thought of the boat and pushed it back down inside him. He had to keep it safe, as far away from the Lizard as he could.

"If I want, I charge you double what I charge everyone else. I make sure you spend your life rotting in this junk heap." He took a step back. "Poof," he said, clicking his fingers. "Just like that I make you disappear. Nobody know any different. You understand?"

Mico nodded, fear clenching his insides like a snake.

"Good. Now get out my sight."

131

20

Mico was still thinking about the Lizard as he headed to his tent. It had been stupid of him to stop like that. He could have walked straight past and the Lizard wouldn't have known any different. But he'd called attention to himself. The thought made him uneasy.

He pushed it aside and focused instead on the boat. It didn't matter what the Lizard said. Until that morning his future had been like a brick wall, solid and unyielding. Now there was a crack running across it. Streams of light shone through the chinks, bathing him in a yellow glow. Leila was right. They could fix it. They had to.

When he reached his tent, he found Hassan outside boiling water over a little metal stove. A scarf was securely wrapped around his face. The sight struck Mico with a sudden pang of guilt. He'd left this morning to see Leila when he should have stayed.

Something had crawled into Hassan's blanket some nights ago and his face was covered in bites. They hadn't been too bad to begin with, but now they were blotchy and filled with pus. He'd been hiding in the tent for days, too afraid to be seen. He hadn't even gone to his French classes. Mico had tried to cheer him up as best he could, but his words were like rain hitting stone. Anything he said just trickled off.

Just then Hassan caught sight of him. Pulling his scarf down a fraction, he beckoned Mico closer.

"What do you think?" he asked, motioning to the stove.

Without meaning to, Mico found himself staring. In the dimness of the tent it had been hard to tell but out in the daylight it was obvious Hassan was suffering. Only a few of the bites were still intact. The rest had been scratched raw. They glowed across his face like angry suns.

Hassan jiggled the water and clicked his tongue in exasperation.

"Not much of a flame," said Mico, tearing his gaze away. The stove was missing a leg. It wobbled precariously as he squatted down.

"Where'd you get it?"

"Omar."

"He gave it to you?" said Mico in surprise.

"I borrowed it," answered Hassan. "Thought I could steam this—" he pointed emphatically to his face, "away. If this water ever boils. Come *on*." He rattled the top of the stove. The tiny flame at the bottom sputtered and died.

"Shit. That's the fifth time that's happened."

"Why don't you go to the clinic?" suggested Mico, as Hassan relit it. "I'm sure they'll be able to give you something."

"And stand for hours in that queue?"

Mico didn't reply. They watched in silence as the

water started to get hotter. A thin curl of steam began to rise upwards. Then, without warning, the flame fluttered and died again. Hassan let out a stream of foreign words and kicked the stove away. The water slopped against the ground and vanished into the soil.

"I could have drunk that," Mico almost started to say, then stopped. Hassan had his head in his hands.

"This place," he murmured. "This bloody place."

Mico stared at him uncertainly. He had never seen Hassan like this before.

"It's going to be all right," he said.

Hassan made a soft moaning sound. With a jolt of alarm, Mico realised he was crying.

"Just look at me."

As Hassan moved his head up, Mico noted, for the first time, the dull circles rimmed beneath his eyes. His hair hung in filthy, listless strands, but worst of all were the bites, swollen like rancid fruit.

"You don't look that bad," he lied.

"How will I become an actor now? They'll take one look at my face and send me packing. First it was Razi. Then the Doctor. Now it's my turn. This place, Mico. It's killing me. Maybe Sy was right. The governments don't give a damn about us. They don't care if we live or die. We're overflow. Stuck in this junk heap. That's why they never give us a second look. We might as well be invisible."

He sniffed and took a deep breath.

"God. I'm losing it. If things don't change soon, I'll try swimming the Channel myself."

"Funny," said Mico, attempting a smile. Only they both knew Hassan wasn't joking.

It was almost evening by the time Leila came. Mico was alone. Sy and Hassan had left a while back to attend a protest meeting against the French government. It had been organised by a man called Suzo. He'd arrived in the camp a month ago with a swagger as big as a house. Mico had seen him a few times, smoking outside his tent with a ring of skinny rat-faced men. He didn't know what they saw in him.

His thoughts strayed back to Hassan. Over the afternoon, his mood seemed to have improved. Mico had coaxed the stove to life and Hassan had sat beside it, leaning his head over the water until it turned cold. Then he'd washed his face. It seemed to help. He'd even managed a couple of jokes. But there was no doubt something in him had changed. They all had, in their own way. Hassan's transformation, though, seemed to be headed in one direction. It was as if he'd given up hope of ever getting out of the camp. Mico knew that was dangerous. A person could learn to live without food or shoes. But without hope you had nothing.

He was still thinking about it when Leila arrived.

"Vegetable rice," she declared buoyantly, handing him a tub. "Some bibs were handing it out at the front of the camp. I saved you some."

Mico took the food without comment. His stomach felt like lead.

"It looks like mud but it tastes pretty good. I'd give anything for some chicken, though. Aysha says I shouldn't think about it but how can you stop yourself thinking? She might as well tell me to stop breathing—"

"I want to tell Hassan about the boat," said Mico

135

suddenly. The words came out in a single, breathless spurt. They remained in the air for a moment, crackling and sparking like the brightest of pinwheels.

Leila frowned, unsure if he was joking.

"Why?" she said finally.

"I want him to come with us."

"Don't be stupid, Mico. You know he can't."

"Why not?"

"The boat's not big enough. He won't fit."

"We have to find a way," said Mico stubbornly. "I don't care how."

"What's wrong with you?" She looked puzzled. "You didn't say anything about this before."

"I'm saying it now."

"But — " Leila was fighting to keep her voice steady. Mico saw the first glimmer of fear creep into her eyes.

"I know how you feel. When I walked through the camp today I thought the same. We'll be leaving all these people behind. But we don't have a choice. We can't take everyone. Today it's Hassan. Tomorrow you'll want to take someone else."

"He was talking about swimming the Channel."

"Just because he said it doesn't mean he would."

"I found it," Mico persisted.

"And I dug it up. It's *our* secret, Mico. You can't tell anyone."

"Fine. But if we're going to fix it, we're taking Hassan with us."

Leila pursed her lips.

"What if I refuse?"

Mico said nothing.

"I won't be able to fix it on my own." Her tone cracked suddenly. "We can't just leave it there." She twisted her hair violently in her fingers as she spoke. "We're supposed to be friends."

Mico took a deep breath. Guilt coiled inside him. He found he could not look at Leila. He could not bear the accusation that was etched like a brand onto her face.

"I'm sorry," he said quietly. "But I can't leave him behind."

Leila shook her head.

"I thought—" she began. Then she shut her eyes and bit her lip as if she was trying not to cry. The effort was too much, however. Gasping slightly, she stood up and stumbled out of the tent.

"I'm sorry," whispered Mico into the silence. He'd thought he was doing the right thing but how could something right feel so wrong? For a moment he was tempted to go after her, to tell her he'd changed his mind but how could he without betraying Hassan? Hassan, who had looked out for him long before Leila arrived.

It was as if he was standing on a riverbank watching his two friends drown. No matter what he did, he couldn't save one without hurting the other. The realisation was too awful to bear. Before he could stop himself, Mico was crying. His body rocked with the force of his tears. He cried for his home, his family, for Leila and Hassan, for the Doctor, Razi, for a future too painful to think about. Then he curled up into a ball and screamed into his blanket until there was no more voice left in him, until, at last, he fell asleep.

21

Mico saw nothing of Leila in the days that followed. He assumed she had sought refuge in her tent and he was glad for it. Seeing her would only have reminded him about the boat. Despite what he'd said he was having a hard time forgetting about it. He had tried not to, but it didn't work. The harder he tried the harder it became. The boat ate at his thoughts like an insect, invading his dreams so that once or twice he'd woken with his arms sculling the air.

In some ways, he was grateful for the protest. Hassan hadn't stopped talking about it since the meeting. Even Sy was looking forward to it.

"This will show the government," he said over and over again. "All we're asking is to be treated right. It's time they help us."

On the evening of the protest, Hassan was crouched outside the tent, putting the final touches to a banner. He had bartered the cloth and paint from another tent.

"What do you think?" he said, adjusting the scarf around his face. His bites still hadn't healed. Mico peered at the words: HUMAN RIGHTS FOR ALL.

"That's it?"

"It's not enough?"

"I suppose." Mico shrugged. "You really think this protest is going to work?"

"Not straight away. But it's a start. That's what Suzo says. He thinks we've got lazy. We sit here and do nothing and that's why the governments ignore us."

"What if the police stop you?"

"Why would they? It's a peaceful protest. We're just walking up to the port." He hit him playfully on the shoulder. "You're coming with us, right?"

Mico hesitated. Then he nodded. It wasn't as if he had anything better to do.

A huge crowd of men had gathered at the front of the camp by the time they arrived.

"Where's the women?" said Mico.

"Suzo didn't want them coming," said Hassan.

"Why not?"

Before Hassan could reply, a loud murmur rose up around them. Mico watched as Suzo stood onto a crate to address the crowd. He had a long face and thin crafty eyes.

"My friends," he began. His voice was thick and hoarse. "Thank you for coming. Today we march out in search of our rights. The governments have slept long enough. It is time they sit up and take notice." He paused and looked steadily at them. "We have been patient but now is the time for action."

As he spoke, Mico saw an enormous gob of spit fly out of his mouth into the audience. Nobody else

139

seemed to notice. He felt a shiver run through him as Suzo stepped off the crate. It wasn't a cold evening, but he pulled his jacket closer around his shoulders and tightened his grip on the banner. He was wedged comfortably between Hassan and Sy, but as they set off he couldn't help wishing Leila was with him. The thought made him unexpectedly sad. He knew she'd never speak to him again.

Through the town they went. People stopped and stared. Some looked out their windows. Others locked their doors. *You don't need to be scared of us*, Mico wanted to shout. *We're just like you.*

Suzo's plan had been to lead them to the port, but as they turned towards it they saw a line of police already waiting for them. Suzo raised his hand and called the crowd to a halt. For several moments, nobody moved or said anything. Mico licked his lips. Though they were standing outside, he suddenly felt hopelessly trapped, as if he was locked in a room without air. The silence was so great he could hear every single little noise – the scrape of a shoe against the ground, the waves crashing nearby, his own heartbeat, everything wound up like a clock, waiting…

Suzo stepped forward and walked across to the officers. Mico felt Hassan stiffen beside him. They were too far away to hear what was being said but it was clear from the officer's hand movements that he wanted them to go back. After a few minutes, Suzo shrugged and turned back towards them. Mico saw him glance across to his rat-faced followers.

With a near imperceptible movement, he lowered his head. Almost simultaneously a rock whizzed through the air and landed on an officer's face. There was a brief holler of triumph then the air was filled with rocks. Within moments the rocks were followed by men.

"We have to get out of here," yelled Mico but his voice was carried away in the rush of people sweeping past him. Out of the corner of his eye he saw the police officers press together, shields ready. Mico twisted around. With a start, he realised Hassan and Sy were no longer beside him. Before he knew what was happening he was being pulled forwards by the crowd, the men moving as one giant wave to the horizon ahead.

A hollow thud reverberated through the air as the two groups made contact. Body met body. Fist met stick. Black uniforms against a maelstrom of rags. Dropping the banner, Mico wrestled a pathway through the tide. Faces tore past him. Hot breath. A sweaty hand. Then somehow he was at the edge of the street, pressed up against a wall as the scuffle continued around him.

Just then he caught sight of Suzo. Somehow he'd managed to get hold of an officer's stick and was thrashing it around with glee. Even from that distance, Mico could see how much he was enjoying it. A wave of hatred surged through him. This was his fault. All that talk of peaceful protest and this was what he'd wanted all along. Not justice, but a chance to get even.

Mico turned away in disgust. A few moments later, he spotted Hassan and Sy. The two of them were locked in a fight with a pair of uniforms. With a sickening lurch in his stomach, Mico saw that Hassan was bleeding from the side of his head. Sy was pounding his fist against an officer's shield like his life depended on it. And their faces... Mico had lived with those faces for months only now they were unrecognisable. There was a madness etched in their features he'd never seen before.

"Mico!"

His head shot round. Through the chaos a voice was calling his name.

"Over here! Mico!"

For one inexplicable second he thought it was Esther. Then he saw Leila's head disappear behind somebody's shoulder. She resurfaced almost at once, gasping like a fish. The scarf she had used to hide her face straggled wildly around her, caught in the strap of her rucksack.

At that moment the air exploded. From everywhere at once: the sound of sirens. A second later, two police vans hurtled to a stop in front of them. A surge of black uniforms cascaded out onto the street. They moved like wolves, shields and sticks snapping at their heels. Shouts of retreat flooded the air as the men began to turn and run.

Mico looked back at Leila and saw her eyes widen in panic. He stepped forward only to be thrown back against the wall. Coughing painfully, he staggered up in time to see a group of officers pushing Suzo to the floor. A rush of panic seized him as he scanned the throng for Hassan and Sy. Where were they?

At last he spotted them. Sy had thrown Hassan over his shoulders and was pushing his way through the crowd. Leila had seen him too. Struggling to stay upright, she raised her arm and waved for help. Sy slowed momentarily – long enough for Mico to see the recognition on his features – then swept straight past her.

Leila turned back to look at Mico and promptly disappeared under a swathe of movement. Barely thinking, Mico dived head first into the torrent. Everything flew past him in a blur.

"Leila!"

He could barely hear himself. With every step forward he was pummelled another two steps back.

"Leila! Where are you?"

It was impossible. He couldn't even see her rucksack. How had he missed it in the first place? And Sy – Mico couldn't think of Sy, not yet.

"Leila!"

Mico swore as an elbow hit him in the face. He needed to get out of here, but he couldn't leave her behind. Suddenly there she was, not a metre away from him – part kneeling, part standing, her rucksack held before her like a shield. Summoning every ounce of strength in his body Mico threw himself towards her. Their hands met.

"Hold on," he bellowed, pulling her upwards. Leila shook her head and pointed to her foot. A bright red stain was blossoming around her ankle. It was the first time Mico had seen her frightened.

Without a word he lifted her onto his back. Together they tumbled through the diminishing troop of people. Not far behind drummed the swift leather of the officers' boots. Mico gasped in pain. His legs and shoulders were burning already. They weren't going to make it back to the camp, not without getting arrested. They needed a hiding place.

"There," hissed Leila in his ear as if she'd read his mind. Mico followed the line of her finger. Less than ten steps away someone had left their front gate open and beyond it – like a lighthouse rising up on the horizon – was an overgrown garden. Filled with dark spaces to hide them from view.

Without a moment's hesitation, he hurtled through the gate. Leila cried out in pain as they toppled onto the grass.

"Quickly," said Mico, dragging her deeper into the undergrowth. But he needn't have worried. Nobody had noticed them. The two of them sat in silence, cowering among the bushes as the stampede coursed past them.

22

They were still in the garden hours later. In the distance the air buzzed with the faint chatter of a police blockade. Mico had thought the officers would leave soon, but now he wasn't sure. What if they stayed the whole night?

He glanced anxiously at Leila. She hadn't once complained, but he knew she was hurting. An inspection of her foot had revealed a thick gash, almost as deep as it was wide. They had mopped the worst of the blood with some leaves, but she needed a doctor. Only they couldn't leave without the risk of being spotted.

At least the house was empty. Mico had feared the noise on the street would disturb the owners, but no lights had turned on, no curious faces had peered out. Clearly the residents were away. Beside him, Leila shivered. He frowned. That was the problem with French summers; they were so damn cold.

"We need to get inside," he said. "We'll freeze if we stay out here."

Leila shook her head. Her eyes glittered with pain.

"We can't go back yet. The police might see us."

"I wasn't talking about the camp."

"What, then? The house will be locked."

"We've got to try."

Keeping an eye out for any uniforms, he helped her towards the house. The front door and windows were shut.

"I told you," Leila muttered.

"Let's check round the side."

The back of the house was barred by a chained wooden gate.

"I might be able to get it open from the other side," said Mico.

"I can't follow you up there," gasped Leila as he shimmied to the top. She put a hand on the fence, fighting to stay upright.

"Give me a second," came Mico's voice from the other side. "The lock's rusted."

A minute later there was the clang of a bolt. Mico threw open the gate just in time to see Leila collapse to the floor. He stared dumbly at her for a moment. She was still conscious, but her breathing was heavy and tired.

"Aysha," she began. "Is. Going."

Panting like a dog.

"To."

Licking her dry lips.

"Be. So. Mad."

Mico shook his head.

"You wait there," he murmured. "I'll find us a way in."

His voice stuck in his throat as he spoke. Without waiting for a reply he turned and ran towards the back of the house. He rattled the door handle. Nothing. He hammered the wood. No luck. In frustration he picked up a nearby flowerpot and smashed it against the glass. A crack appeared in the pane. He brought it down again, harder this time, no longer caring if anyone heard.

Glass splintered the air. In the silence of the night it sounded as loud as an explosion. Pulling his sleeve down over his wrist, Mico slipped his hand through the hole and felt for the key, grateful that the owners hadn't installed an alarm system.

Once inside he switched on a light and ran back to Leila. Trying not to notice the coldness of her skin, he lifted her into the air. Her rucksack bounced against his stomach as he carried her indoors.

The house had clearly been empty for a while. A thick layer of dust sat across the furniture and the air smelled stale. It was cold, too, but in the living room Mico found a fireplace and a basket of logs. The matches were in the kitchen.

It took him a few attempts to get the fire lit but as soon as it was done the house didn't seem nearly so unfriendly. The hiss and spit of the flames gave Mico enough courage to venture upstairs. A search of the bedrooms revealed pillows, blankets and, tucked away at the back of a chest of drawers, a first-aid kit.

He carried everything downstairs then he went back to the kitchen to heat some water. Leila glanced at him curiously as he re-entered the room. Some of the colour was already returning to her cheeks.

"What's that for?" she said, nodding at the bowl of water in his hands.

"We've got to clean your foot before you can put the bandages on it."

147

Leila stared at him suspiciously.

"Trust me. Chickens are bastard biters. Back home, I got cut all the time."

"Fine, but I'll do it myself," declared Leila firmly, taking the bowl from him. "I might be hurt but I'm not completely useless."

Mico shrugged, but inside he was smiling. The fire was clearly doing its job.

"I'm going to look for some food. I'm starving."

"I'll have a lamb curry," Leila replied, dabbing the edge of a towel against her skin. "Extra spicy. And a slice of *basbousa*."

The fridge was empty, but the cupboard under the sink was stacked with tins of food. Mico pulled out three at random and ripped them open. A few minutes later, he re-entered the room with cold tomato soup, chickpeas and fruit custard.

Leila drew a sharp intake of breath as he put down the tray.

"One lamb curry and a slice of *basbousa*," said Mico triumphantly.

For some time the room was filled with the sounds of chomping and slurping. Only when the last of the custard had been licked clean from their bowls did they finally sit back.

"That's the best thing I've eaten in months," said Leila. Her voice dropped. "I wish Aysha was here. She'd love this."

"We can take some tins back for her," said Mico. He couldn't remember the last time he'd been warm and full. It felt good, better than he'd have thought possible. He threw a couple more logs onto the fire. The flames sputtered and popped.

"Why were you at the protest?" Leila asked.

"Hassan asked me to come. What about you? I thought girls weren't allowed."

"I was curious."

Mico raised his eyebrows.

"You could have been killed."

"So could you."

They were silent for a moment. Mico glanced at Leila and wondered if she was thinking the same as him.

"I guess Sy didn't recognise you," he said.

"No."

Leila didn't meet his eye. They both knew the truth. It made Mico sick to think that Sy had just left her there.

His gaze moved to her foot where a thin line of red was just visible beneath the bandage.

"Did Aysha know you were coming?"

Leila made a face. "You know what she's like. She'd have barred me in with her stomach if she'd guessed. I told her I was coming to meet you. She was starting to wonder why you hadn't been round."

She trailed off and looked down at her foot, inspecting the bandage with an expression of intense concentration.

"Have you been to see the boat?"

The question was out of Mico's mouth before he could stop himself. He regretted it almost at once.

Leila didn't even look up.

"What's the point?" she said dully. "I can't do anything with it. Not on my own." She hissed in pain as she moved her foot. But she did not look at him. She would not look. There was a long silence. Mico cleared his throat.

"I'm going to get some water. Do you want any?"

Leila shook her head, unable to meet his eye. When

149

he returned from the kitchen, she was flipping through her sketchbook. A faint smile played at the corners of her mouth. Mico hung back, unwilling to disturb her. She must have sensed him watching because she suddenly spoke.

"Sit down if you want to see."

The first picture she showed him was a house. It had yellow shutters on the windows and a pretty yellow door.

"That's where we used to live," said Leila. "Me, Aysha and Jahir." She tapped the sketchbook. "He bought me this on my birthday. 'We all carry our own beauty inside us,' he said. 'It's your job to spot it.' Aysha was always teasing him. She said he should have been an artist not a doctor."

She turned the page. The next painting was of a wide, open street. It had houses on one side and brightly coloured shop fronts on the other. In front of one of the shops stood a stout, bearded man.

"Who's that?" asked Mico.

"Adil the butcher. He was funny. Every time I went into his shop he'd teach me a new swear word."

Leila smiled.

"Aysha was furious when she found out."

As they continued through the pages, the pictures became greyer, thinner until there was no colour left in them at all.

"Ran out of paint," said Leila sadly.

The most recent picture was drawn in pencil.

It showed three figures in a boat. They were looking out towards the horizon with their hands raised to their head. Leila had drawn them from behind so Mico couldn't see their faces but he didn't need to. He already knew who they were.

"You didn't finish it?" he said.

Leila looked embarrassed.

"I started it before—"

She snapped the book shut.

"It doesn't matter now. I'm tired. Let's get some sleep."

✮ ✯ ✮

The police blockade disappeared early the next afternoon. As soon as they arrived back at camp they were met by a furious Aysha, who, upon seeing her sister, promptly burst into tears. Unfortunately, the tears dried up fast when they told her what had happened.

"Where did you go?" she exclaimed shrilly.

Leila threw Mico an apologetic glance.

"To the protest," she mumbled.

"I don't believe you, Leila. I told you to stay away from it, didn't I? I knew what would happen." She said something in another language and stamped her shoe against the ground. "It's bad enough us having to live like this without me worrying about you as well. Do you have any idea what you put me through last night? I had all these terrible ideas going through my mind. I went and asked round his tent—" She gestured at Mico who shrank back against the wall, trying to make himself as small as possible. "—but it was empty. Went this morning and that man, Syed, told me to leave. Said he had no idea where you might be and that I should keep a closer eye on you. Irresponsible, he called me. Me!"

Leila exchanged a helpless look with Mico. Aysha was lumbering around the tent like a whale, swatting a flannel at an army of invisible insects. The more she spoke the faster the flannel whipped through the air.

"I'm sorry, Aysh," said Leila. "I didn't mean to get hurt. If I'd known it was going to be dangerous, I wouldn't have gone."

Aysha snorted.

"Don't lie to me. You would have jumped at the chance. No, it's my fault. I've given you too much freedom. But not anymore. From now on, you won't be leaving this tent without me."

"You can't do that."

For the first time, Leila's voice rose louder than her sister's.

"I'm not a child."

"You behave like one."

"But—"

"I don't want to hear another word."

Aysha put her hands on her hips. The movement made her look twice as big as she already was.

"We're going to the clinic to get your foot checked up and then we are coming straight back. Do you understand?"

Leila stuck out her lip.

"You're not giving me any choice," she objected.

Aysha ignored her and turned on Mico.

"I suppose you went too?"

He nodded reluctantly.

"Leave him alone, Aysh," snapped Leila. "Mico got me out of there. If it wasn't for him I wouldn't have made it back."

"That's not true," said Mico quickly. Aysha's face had turned red. She looked like she was going to explode.

"I think you'd best leave," she said icily. With surprising agility, she grabbed hold of Mico's collar and dragged him outside.

"Can I come later?" he asked.

But Aysha had already gone back inside.

23

Mico stomped back to his tent in a foul mood. As always the camp was a muddle of sound and colour. An old lady sat hunched over a cooking pot. Children shrieked and jumped in the dirt as their mothers sat and watched. Men talked and spat and smoked.

Mico hardly noticed. He was cross that Leila had got hurt and crosser still that Aysha blamed him for it. Even worse, he knew it was his fault. If he'd agreed to fix the boat Leila probably wouldn't have been at the protest.

As he drew up to the tent, he heard a burst of angry voices flood into the air. Hassan and Sy seemed to be in the middle of an argument. He slowed, uncertain if he should enter or wait for them to finish.

"You shouldn't have left him behind."

Mico drew closer, suddenly curious. They were talking about him.

"Actually, it's my fault," continued Hassan. "I shouldn't have made him go."

"You didn't know what would happen," Sy retorted. "It was meant to be a peaceful protest."

"What if he's been arrested? If he talks to the police—"

"He won't. Anyway the police have no proof who was there. Mico will be the only one in trouble."

"But if he mentions our names—" Hassan sighed. "He should never have been allowed to leave home in the first place. He's just a child. What does he know about the real world?"

Mico clenched his fists. He had heard enough. Hassan was still talking as he stepped inside. Almost at once he fell silent, his expression frozen in surprise. He looked so comical that if Mico hadn't been so angry he might have laughed.

"You back then?"

Sy was the first to speak. He had a jagged, diamond-shaped bruise across his eye. It made him appear rougher, dangerous even.

"Looks like it," replied Mico.

Hassan threw him an anxious look. He was sitting up against a pillow with a bandage tied on his head.

"Hey, Mico, I'm sorry," he said. "We shouldn't have left you like that." He smiled half-heartedly.

"Some crazy stuff went down last night. I guess we all got a bit carried away."

Mico said nothing.

"Where did you go anyway?"

"Why do you care?"

"I understand if you're angry…"

"Do you?"

"It was an accident," interrupted Sy with a low growl. "We lost you."

"And Leila? Was she an accident too?"

155

Sy's eyes flickered in surprise.

"Yeah," said Mico. "I saw you."

"What are you talking about?"

Hassan was watching the two of them in puzzlement.

"You didn't tell him?" Mico smiled mirthlessly. "Sy left Leila behind at the protest."

"What?"

Sy's mouth twisted in scorn.

"*Sha*, Hassan. Don't look at me like that. The girl came of her own free will. Her sister should have kept a closer eye on her. She wasn't my responsibility."

"She was hurt," said Mico, his voice rising dangerously. "She could have been trampled to death."

"Then she should have been more careful."

"Is that why you lied to her sister when she came? Or were you too scared to tell her the truth?"

Sy's eyes narrowed. The bruise on his face glinted menacingly.

"If you've got something to say, Mico, say it. Don't play games with me."

"All right. You're a coward."

Sy was on him in a flash. Before Mico could resist he was being lifted into the air.

"Say that again," snarled Sy.

Mico could hardly breathe, so strong was the grip around his throat.

"That's enough, Sy. Put him down."

Sy didn't move.

"I mean it," said Hassan sharply. "You're going to kill him."

A moment later, Mico felt the grasp around his neck loosen.

"You better watch that mouth of yours," said Sy,

lowering him back to the floor. "It's getting too big for you to carry around."

With a final glance at Hassan, he left.

Mico coughed.

"Truth hurts," he said, sitting up. "Not my fault I touched a nerve."

"You shouldn't have called him a coward."

"Why? Because it's true?"

Hassan shook his head, wincing a little at the movement.

"He got me to the clinic in time. Doctor said I was lucky. If I'd lost any more blood it could have been serious."

"That's not the point," said Mico. "He shouldn't have left Leila behind." A sudden burst of anger flashed through him. "Why are you sticking up for him anyway? Because he saved you?"

Hassan shrugged.

"I care about him," he said quietly, not meeting his eye.

Mico stared at him, suddenly remembering what Sara had said all those weeks ago. He hadn't understood then, but now he did.

"You don't have to say anything," said Hassan into the silence.

"Has it always – I mean, have you always…?"

"Yes."

"And Sy?"

"It's – difficult for him," replied Hassan dully.

"He doesn't give a damn about anyone else," said Mico. "He just wants to earn enough money to get to England."

Hassan sighed.

"He could have left me at the protest, Mico. But he didn't."

"That doesn't mean he cares."

Hassan didn't reply. He was hunched over himself, blood peeling at the corners of his bandage. He looked so sad and sorry for himself that Mico wasn't even angry at him anymore.

"You couldn't have found anyone else?" he said flatly.

A ghost of a smile twitched at the corners of Hassan's mouth.

"Nobody's perfect."

"No," said Mico, touching a hand to his throat. "No, they're not."

24

A short while later, Mico found himself wandering through the camp. He'd left the tent soon after his argument with Sy. Hassan hadn't tried stopping him. He hadn't even asked where he was going. After the protest something had changed between them. They both knew it. Though they were still talking there was an unspoken silence wedged beneath their words. It was as if, after all these months, they'd found themselves on two separate sides of a wall.

Mico could never forgive Sy for abandoning Leila. Yet deep down he knew that Hassan could. Hassan could forgive Sy anything.

And Mico hated him for it.

He walked around for a while, hands in pockets, trying to ignore the police officers. They had started patrolling the camp after the protest. They moved in a single pack, masks on faces, batons in hands. On their boots they wore a sheet of plastic so the soles didn't get dirty. They didn't make eye contact, didn't speak, but everyone knew why they were there.

Their presence, however, had little effect on some of the camp's residents. As Mico passed Shakeel's tent he saw him crouched outside with a couple of other boys, trying to fix some kind of generator. Strangely, he didn't feel envious of them anymore; in fact, as he stopped and watched them inspect the wiring, he was struck by an overwhelming sense of fear. Was this to be their future? To scrape in the dirt, hoping to find a way to turn it into gold?

He thought back to what the Lizard had said. Even if he did somehow find the money to pay him there was no way of knowing if he'd actually put him on a truck, no guarantee he'd get across the Channel. Uncle Abu had told him to find a better life for himself. But how? Tomorrow was as unpredictable as the wind and he was like a wingless bird struggling in its midst.

With a final glance at Shakeel, he turned away. He didn't think he was heading in any particular direction until he was in sight of the trees. All of a sudden he was filled with a great urgency. He doubled his pace, eventually breaking into a run. His heart thudded painfully as he whipped through the foliage. Doubts roared in his mind. What if the boat was gone? What if someone else had found it?

By the time he entered the hollow he was convinced he'd find it empty. But as he cleared the leaves away he saw the boat was still there, exactly as they'd left it. He sketched the outline of the bird again as if to reassure himself it wasn't a dream. Leila had been right. Apart from the hole, the rest of the boat was in good shape. A thorough clean would be enough to get it looking almost respectable.

He clambered onto the prow and stretched out his arms either side of him. He closed his eyes, imagining the swell of a current beneath him. When he opened his eyes again, he found he was smiling.

It was approaching dusk by the time he went to visit Leila. Aysha glanced up as he entered. Mico hesitated, certain she would tell him to leave. Instead, she motioned him to sit.

"Good news," she said, flicking a glance at Leila's newly bandaged foot. "The doctors said it's just a cut." The relief in her voice was audible. "Should heal quickly, but they've covered it up so it doesn't get infected."

"I'll die of boredom before then," muttered Leila sourly.

Aysha ignored her and heaved herself to her feet. She picked up a pot and a small packet of uncooked rice.

"I'm going to make dinner," she said. "Next door have a stove. They're letting me use it in exchange for half the rice. There should be enough for three of us."

Mico started to decline.

"I wasn't asking." Aysha broke into an unexpected smile. "Today is a good day. We have rice. And a roof over our heads. There is much to be grateful for."

Mico thought he saw a scowl cross Leila's features, but it was gone so quickly he wondered if he'd imagined it.

"I won't be long," Aysha continued. She nodded at Leila. "In the meantime, try cheering her up. She's been looking like a constipated pig all day."

Leila snorted derisively. As soon as Aysha had left, she exploded.

"She's being a total mule," she said, keeping her

voice low. "When we came back this afternoon, she went to make an appointment with Judge Specs."

"Why?"

"Why do you think? She's thinking about staying in France."

Mico blinked.

"What about England?"

"She said she doesn't care anymore. The baby's going to be due soon and we can't be here when she comes. It *will* be a girl," she continued, noting the look on Mico's face. "I just know it."

"But—"

Mico couldn't even think what to say. Leila's words had opened up a great chasm inside him and he felt as if he was standing on the very edge. *What about me?* he wanted to ask. But somehow the question couldn't quite form on his lips.

"You can't stay in France," he said finally. He was relieved to hear Leila agree with him.

"That's what I told her. We don't even know the language. They only taught us English in school not French. How will we talk to anyone? But she's not listening to me—"

"I went to see the boat," blurted Mico suddenly. The statement took Leila by surprise. That night, in the house, she had hidden her feelings well but this time she was not quick enough. A flash of accusation and pain darted across her features.

"Why?" she asked quietly.

"I want to fix it."

Leila shook her head.

"I told you," she said. "We can't take Hassan with us."

Mico took a deep breath. The realisation of what

162

he was about to say stung, more than he would have thought possible.

"Hassan won't come," he said.

"How do you know?" retorted Leila. Her eyes widened. "Did you tell him?"

"No."

Leila was watching him with a distinct look of suspicion.

"I never told him," snapped Mico.

"Then how do you know?"

Mico thought back to that afternoon. He could not tell her the truth, not without betraying Hassan's trust.

"I just do," he said. "Do you want to fix it or not?"

"You know I do."

"The worst damage is the hole. We're going to need some wood to fix it. And a hammer. Nails."

"Do you really want to do this?" said Leila. "Last time you—"

"I've changed my mind," interrupted Mico firmly.

"How do I know you won't change it again?"

"I won't." He dug his hand into his pocket and held it out. In his palm was a single white feather. He had found it in the boat and brought it with him. He hoped Leila would see it as he did. As a symbol of faith. A sign that they were meant to fix it.

"I promise."

Leila picked up the feather and sucked in air through her teeth, contemplating. At last, she took out her sketchbook and slipped the feather inside.

"What else do we need?" she asked.

"Food."

"Water."

"Paint to cover the cracks. I know where Hassan

163

threw that pot they used for the banner. There must still be some left in there."

"Something waterproof," said Leila. "In case it rains."

"Where are we going to get this stuff?"

"We can check the rubbish around the camp. There's plenty lying around. Must be some bits we can use."

Mico sat back and drummed his fingers on his knees.

"Nobody will have thrown away a hammer. And we're not going to find any food."

Leila was silent for a moment. Then her eyes lit up.

"What about the house? You said there were more tins in the kitchen. And wasn't there a shed in the garden? We might find some tools in there."

"Maybe," admitted Mico grudgingly.

In truth, he had already had the same idea but it didn't feel right to rob from the same people twice. Leila seemed to read his mind.

"It's not stealing, Mico." She grinned impishly. "Think of it as charity."

"What are you two whispering about?"

They looked up, startled. They had been so caught up in their conversation that neither one of them had heard Aysha come in.

"You're up to something," she said, narrowing her eyes.

Leila put her hands up. "You're right. We were going to dig a tunnel to get me out of here. Thought you wouldn't notice."

Aysha rolled her eyes.

"Rice will be a while yet," she said, manoeuvring herself to the floor. "They sent me back to rest while it cooks." Suddenly she squealed, her hand shooting down to her stomach.

164

"Is it the baby?" asked Leila, flustered.

A smile crossed Aysha's features as she looked up at them.

"First kick," she whispered.

"Let me feel," said Leila, moving beside her. She put a hand on her dress. Mico hung back, embarrassed.

"Come on," said Aysha, holding out her hand.

Reddening slightly, Mico moved up next to Leila and let her guide his hand onto Aysha's stomach. He could feel the soft rise and fall of her breath, gentle like the whisper of leaves.

"I can't feel anything," muttered Leila crossly.

"Stop talking and wait," said Aysha.

Leila opened her mouth to argue, but just then they felt it. A kick. Tiny, but surprisingly hard and strong.

"There it is!" cried Leila in excitement, throwing her arms around her sister and hugging her tight.

"She's a fighter, Aysh. She's going to be a fighter like us."

"She's a miracle," murmured Mico softly. When he looked up he saw that Leila was smiling at him.

"What?"

"You said she."

"Yeah." He leant back on the balls of his feet and grinned. "I guess I did."

25

The next morning, Mico began searching through the camp's rubbish. Piles and piles of it were scattered around the edge of the tents. Mountains of bottles, walls of wet cardboard, stacks of empty cans and that was just the stuff he could see. The more he explored the more he realised how impossible a task he had taken on. There was so much rubbish he felt as if he was wading through the guts of some huge scavenging monster that had staggered into the camp to die.

"Won't take long," he said, mimicking Leila's voice as he clambered behind the tents. "Must be something we can use, Mico."

Grunting, he threw aside some empty food packaging and was instantly attacked by an army of flies. With a sharp cry, he lurched backwards and tumbled into a heap of black bags. It was like drowning in a flood of sewage. He scrambled up, retching and spluttering as the smell clawed through his lungs.

All of a sudden he heard giggling. He looked up to find two girls watching him.

"What you looking at?" he growled.

"You won't find no food to eat der," said one know-ingly.

The other one whispered something in her ear.

"What's she saying?"

"She wanna know if you got burnt by da sun. Is dat why you so black?"

Mico flushed.

"Why don't you come closer and I'll show you?" he yelled, striding forward. The girls squealed and fled. Mico ran a few steps after them then stopped, watching as they disappeared among the tents. He took a deep breath and brushed himself down. Clearly he wasn't going to find anything here. It was time for a change of tactic.

First he found a stick. One that was long enough to allow him to search the rubbish from a distance. Then he went back for his knife. If he'd had tape or rope, he would have just fixed it to the end of the stick. Instead, he had to scratch the blade against the wood to form a spike. He worked quickly, reluctant that Sy or Hassan should return to the tent and see what he was doing.

When he was satisfied it was sharp enough he slipped the knife back in its hiding place and headed for the trees. There was even more rubbish here but armed with his spear, Mico now made much better progress. If any bag looked promising, he could cut it open and poke around its contents from afar.

But after what felt like hours he was still no closer to finding anything. The rubbish was just that: rubbish. The only thing he had found was a rat which had flown into the air like its tail was on fire. Mico had been so surprised he had almost dropped his stick.

Still, he wasn't quite ready to quit.

"What you doing?"

Mico's head shot up. He had been so engrossed in his task he hadn't even realised he had an audience. The Crow was watching him curiously.

"I ask you a question."

Mico swallowed. What should he say?

"You a mute?"

"No."

The Crow stroked his chin. The rings on his fingers glittered blood-red.

"You lost something?"

A look of hunger flitted across his face.

"Valuable, was it? I can help. Four eyes better than two."

Mico leant on his stick. Suddenly he found he was no longer afraid. The Crow was nothing but a scavenger. A shadow, always following in the Lizard's wake. Mico doubted he had the guts to do anything for himself. But if he wanted him to leave, he had to say something.

"I'm hungry," he declared.

The Crow wrinkled his nose in revulsion.

"You looking for food? In this place?"

Mico nodded and held his stick out in the air.

"Will you help?"

"You crazy." The Crow tapped a finger against the side of his head. "Crazy, yes."

Mico bit back a smile as he watched him walk away.

By the afternoon, he was totally fed up. His back and arms ached. He stank. And he *still* hadn't found anything. The Crow was right. He really was crazy.

Throwing the stick aside, he stomped back to his tent. Hassan was already inside. He was still wearing a bandage, but he looked far less pale than he had a few days ago.

"What's the stink?" he enquired.

"I need to borrow a T-shirt," said Mico. "Just for a few hours."

"Help yourself. What have you been doing anyway? Smells like you swam through a pool of shit."

Mico smiled grimly.

"You could say that."

The beach was quiet. Mico slipped off his shoes, rolled up his jeans and waded into the water. It was a warm day with only a slight hint of wind. Far out in the horizon he could see a couple of ships, huge and white like whales.

A wave of hopelessness rushed through him as he watched them. They looked so powerful, so unlike the boat marooned in the trees. Sighing, he removed his T-shirt and swapped it for Hassan's clean one. Then he rinsed his own and slung it over his shoulder. He thought back to what Leila had said. About the house and the shed. Then he thought of the camp. It only took him a few seconds to decide. With a final wistful look at the ships, he headed off before he could change his mind.

The house's front gate was shut. So was the door and the windows. Everything was exactly as they'd left it. Mico waited until the street was clear before slipping inside.

Climbing soundlessly over the back gate, he dropped down into the garden. The shed was padlocked shut. Mico rattled it in frustration. The lock was solid. He needed something strong to break it – like a brick or... His lips curled as he caught sight of the gnome in the flowerbed.

"Sorry," he said, lifting it into the air. The gnome

glared back at him in accusation. Mico raised it above his head. Praying that nobody would hear him, he brought it down onto the lock with a loud *thunk*. He flinched at the noise and glanced at the neighbouring houses. Nothing.

He turned back to the door and hit the lock harder. Then again. And again. With each strike the gnome appeared crosser and crosser. On the fifth attempt, the lock finally gave way.

With a final glance over his shoulder, Mico pushed open the door and stepped inside. The shed was darker than he'd expected. As his eyes adjusted to the dimness, the shadows in front of him began to shift and take shape. A couple of bikes leant against the wall, along with a skateboard and rolled-up carpets. An old TV. Some paint. Hosepipes, rope, boxes.

His eye fell on a pair of shelves. Right on the top sat a toolbox. Hardly daring to hope, Mico hurried forward and lifted it down onto the floor. He crowed in triumph as he threw open the lid. Inside were all the tools they needed and more.

If Leila had been with him she would have taken the whole thing, but Mico knew it would look strange if he walked into camp loaded with such expensive gear. People might start asking questions. Instead, he took only what he thought they'd need – a hammer, a little saw and a few packets of nails. He had only just put the toolbox back when he heard voices behind him.

26

Mico froze. Perhaps the neighbours had spotted him. Or, worse, maybe the house owners were back. Outside the voices were growing louder. They sounded upset. Mico found himself wishing he'd attended more French lessons. At least he'd have known what they were saying.

All of a sudden he heard footsteps drawing towards the shed. Panicking, he glanced around for somewhere to hide. There wasn't much choice. The space was small and exposed, good for a rat, not so good for him.

The footsteps were coming nearer.

Just then he spotted something. At the back, behind a lawnmower, were some kitchen units covered by a sheet. Scrambling to his feet, Mico crawled beneath it and squeezed into a corner. As he pulled the lawnmower in front of him the door opened. Light flooded inside. Wedged into his corner, Mico could make out the vague silhouette of a man. He said something in French and stepped inside. Then, in clipped English, "Hallo? Is anyone here?"

Mico held his breath. After a few moments, the man shut the door. There was a loud dragging noise then footsteps. As soon as he was out of earshot, Mico crept out of his hiding place and tried the door. It didn't budge. He swore. The man must have put something across it. That's what the noise had been.

He spun round, searching for another way out. The shed had a window, but it was too small for him to fit through. He turned back to the door and shook the handle again.

"Come on," he hissed. "Open up."

The door rattled, but stayed firm. Mico kicked it a few times, hoping to dislodge whatever was on the other side. Still nothing. At last, he stepped back. The truth of his situation was only now starting to sink in.

He was trapped. Nobody knew where he was. The last person he'd spoken to was Hassan but he hadn't told him where he was going. Neither had he spoken to Leila. In any case she wasn't allowed out the tent until her foot healed.

A cold rush of fear took hold of him. No-one would look for him here. He was alone. In desperation, he bashed the door with his palm but it was about as effective as stroking it with a feather. Scowling, he slumped back against the door. He'd just have to sit tight. Wait until somebody opened the shed then run for it. If he was fast enough he might get away.

By the time dusk fell, Mico was stiff and hungry. He'd have been cold, too, if he hadn't already found a jacket stuffed behind the bikes. It was miles too big for him, but he'd put it on at once, over both T-shirts, so that he looked like a bear.

Earlier that afternoon he had heard more voices

outside. Unfriendly. Authoritative. Certain they were police, he'd hidden himself again, but nobody had come to the shed. When the voices had gone, he'd crept back out. With nothing else to do he'd decided to explore.

His search proved a good one. Behind some paint pots he had come across a stack of wooden boards. On first glance they'd looked too flimsy for the boat but after dragging them out onto the floor, Mico had changed his mind. It would take some effort but if he cut the wood down to size he could layer it across the hole before hammering it down.

The idea pleased him until he remembered he had no way out of the shed.

"Way to go, Mico," he muttered bitterly. "Trapped like Ma-Kubi."

Ma-Kubi, who had begged the gods to turn her into a fish so that she could swim underwater. They had granted her wish on one condition – that she return to shore when the last rays of sun set over the horizon. But Ma-Kubi forgot. Only at the last moment did she remember their warning. As quickly as she could she raced to the surface. But it was too late. When she emerged from the water the sun had already descended, leaving Ma-Kubi imprisoned in the body of a fish for the rest of her life.

When Ma had told him the story, Mico's first thought was how stupid Ma-Kubi had been. How could she forget? But Mico had behaved just like her. How could he have been so careless? Now they had the boat there was too much to lose. Without money there was no other way to reach England. As for Hassan – Mico felt sick to the stomach when he thought of betraying him. But Hassan would not leave Sy.

And you? said a little voice in his head. If Hassan had

been the one to find the boat would he have shared it with Mico? Or would he only have told Sy?

Mico didn't like to think what the answer might be.

In the camp there was plenty to distract a person but here in the shed the questions kept on coming.

Suddenly tired, he shut his eyes and leant his head against the door. He hoped someone would open it soon. Even the idea of a police cell didn't scare him anymore. At least it would be warm and he'd be given food.

"Mico."

The voice was so unexpected he almost cried out. He caught himself in time and peered into the shadows in front of him.

"Esther?" he whispered.

"Are you in there? It's me, Leila."

She gave a little tap on the door.

"I'm here," said Mico, feeling stupid. His voice sounded dry and unfamiliar. "Can you get me out?"

"What do you think I'm doing?"

Mico heard her grunting with effort. There was the same dragging noise from earlier then the door was pulled open. Leila stared at him, her eyes flaming with a mixture of incredulity and relief.

"Are you crazy?" she hissed. "You came on your own?"

Behind her, Mico could see lights on in the house.

"Lucky I came," Leila was saying. "When Hassan came looking for you, I guessed you might be here. You could have told me—"

"We need to move," interrupted Mico. He was in no mood to hear any accusations. "Someone might have heard you."

Leila's eyes thinned dangerously but she did not argue.

"Here—" He handed her the hammer and saw. "Put them in your rucksack."

"Where are you going?" she whispered as he ducked inside. He was back a few moments later with the boards.

Leila looked dubious.

"Are they enough?"

"Have to be," puffed Mico. "I can't carry anymore."

His gaze fell on her foot, on the bandage peeling away.

"How did you get in?" he asked suddenly.

"Climbed the fence," said Leila. Then, at the consternation on Mico's face, "What? They fixed the lock—"

She was cut off by the sound of barking. She looked at Mico. The noise was coming from the adjacent garden, loud enough to be heard half a street away.

"Come on," said Mico, giving her a shove.

Sensing their movement, the dog began baying like crazy. They heard the rattle of a chain as it threw itself against the fence. Above them, a window opened. A head poked out.

"Run," he exclaimed.

Leila tried. She did. But her foot was still healing and the best she could manage was a jerky limp. They had only just reached the gate when they heard a door opening. Mico twisted round in time to see a man charging towards them. He shouted in French, the words shooting into the air like hailstones.

Mico reacted instinctively. As the man drew closer, he swung round and hit him with the boards. He had meant to aim for his shoulder, but caught the side of his face instead. A sickening thud resounded through the

175

air as wood crunched against bone. With a little yelp, the man fell to the ground.

"Shit," said Mico, bending down over him. The man's eyes were closed. Leila was watching with her mouth open.

"Is he—"

The question was too terrible for her to finish. On the other side of the fence, the dog was howling like something possessed.

"Don't be stupid," said Mico. Fingers trembling a little, he put a hand on the man's chest. Relief flooded through him as he felt it. Right beneath his palm was a slow flicker of life, faint but steady.

"He's not dead," he said, standing up. "Just unconscious."

As he finished speaking, a scream splintered the air. The noise was as sharp as a needle. Even the dog fell silent. In the doorway, still wearing a shockingly pink dressing gown, a woman was pointing her finger at them.

"*Voleurs,*" she cried. "*Police! POLICE!*"

She turned and ran back inside. Right on cue the dog began barking again.

"We need to hurry," said Mico urgently. But Leila was frozen to the spot, her gaze fixed on the man. The side of his head was bleeding.

"I told you. He's alive."

"Shouldn't we help him?"

"And get ourselves arrested?"

"But it's our fault."

Mico couldn't quite believe what he was hearing. Was this the same Leila who had thrown rocks at a stranger? Who had got into a fight over a bike?

"We don't have time," he replied firmly, steering her

176

towards the fence. Leila's face was set in disagreement. She looked back at the man, her expression torn.

"It's not right," she murmured.

In the distance they heard the faint but sure trill of a siren.

"Do you hear that?" said Mico. "If we don't leave right now they'll throw both of us into a cell. Now *hurry up.*"

He put down the boards and crouched down to give Leila a leg-up. Mercifully she did not argue. The siren was growing louder by the second. With some difficulty, Mico climbed up, handed over the boards one by one, then dropped down after them. He must have checked over his shoulder about a hundred times before they finally reached the camp. At every step he expected a police car to pull up alongside them, imagined voices ordering them to stop. But there was nothing, nobody, save for the two of them hurrying along in the gloom.

The camp, when they got there, was quiet. Hardly anyone saw them as they passed between the tents. It was too dark to find the boat so they hid the tools and the boards in some bushes at the edge of the woods.

"Isn't Aysha going to be mad at you?" asked Mico as they headed back to the tents. Leila had been silent the whole way. He wasn't sure if it was because of her foot or if she was still thinking about the man at the house.

"I thought you weren't allowed out till your foot's healed."

"She doesn't know," explained Leila. "You missed the new arrivals. The Ghost-Men brought them a few hours ago. One of the ladies is near us. She's got a baby with her but it's like she's forgotten about him. She

177

just sits in a corner, crying. Doesn't speak. Some of the women are taking it in turns to stay with her. Aysha said it's important not to leave her alone."

She sighed heavily.

"I still think we should have helped that man."

"If we'd helped we'd be in jail right now," replied Mico sourly. "Is that what you want?"

"I'm only saying. We decided to fix the boat. We didn't agree to hurt anyone."

There was an accusation in her voice which Mico didn't like.

"It's not my fault."

"It wasn't his either."

"I didn't mean to hit him like that," growled Mico. "It was an accident." Why wasn't she listening? Couldn't she see that he felt guilty about it too? But Leila's face was etched with uncertainty.

"What if he's hurt bad? The police might come looking for us."

"Then we just have to hope they won't," he said grimly. Leila was clearly unhappy with this answer but she said nothing more. They continued in silence for a few minutes then, tired and exasperated, departed without a word.

Hassan and Sy were both awake when Mico walked into the tent. A single candle gave out the only light, illuminating the whites of their eyes, pale and milky like the stare of ghosts.

"You're back." Hassan looked relieved. "Where'd you go?"

Mico ignored the question and slumped down on his blanket.

"Nice jacket," said Sy.

Mico swore inwardly. He'd forgotten he was wearing it.

"You steal it?"

"Someone gave it to me."

"They *gave* it to you?"

"Some people have a heart."

Sy's face darkened. With a filthy look in Mico's direction, he turned away from them.

"I came looking for you," said Hassan after a short pause. "Leila said she hadn't seen you either."

Mico ignored the question in his voice.

"I got you this."

Hassan held out a bar of chocolate. Without thinking, Mico snatched it from his hand and began wolfing it down. He'd already eaten half of it before it occurred to him that it might be a peace offering, one he was meant to share.

"Haven't eaten since morning," he explained, pretending not to notice Hassan's stare. He knew he was being rude and that he should give him some, but he was too hungry.

"Don't have it all now," said Hassan finally.

He pinched the candle between his fingers, plunging the tent into shadow.

"You'll get stomach ache. Save some for tomorrow."

Tomorrow.

Mico gulped down the last piece of chocolate where it sat like a bullet in his chest. Crunching the wrapper in his hands, he lay down. He should have been happy. He'd got out of the shed without getting arrested. They had the wood to fix the boat. But Leila's words had made him uneasy. More than that he was angry. Angry at Leila for doubting him, angry at himself for hitting the man. Even as he replayed the scene over in his head he still wasn't sure why he'd lashed out that way. It had been pure reflex. He hadn't thought about what he was doing. He had simply reacted.

He closed his eyes, hoping for sleep. Only he couldn't forget the lady's face, the thud as the man had fallen to the ground. Who knew what line the police would take? Assault? Attempted murder? What if Leila was right? What if the man really was hurt?

He opened his eyes and stared into the darkness. Tomorrow loomed back at him like an endless tunnel, an open mouth ready to swallow him whole. Damn it. He turned over onto his side. He should have shared the chocolate.

27

The following afternoon a police car drove into the camp. Mico was one of the first to see it. As soon as he'd woken up he'd made his way over to the entrance. He'd been hanging around for hours. It was silly, but somehow he'd convinced himself that if he stayed here long enough the police might never come. As if, with his mind, he could create a shield that would protect him from the outside world. But he'd been wrong.

He watched with growing agitation as the officers disembarked. It was clear from their uniform that they weren't part of the usual wolf pack. They were here for another reason. Ducking behind a tent, he watched as they moved from one group of residents to another, interrogating, barking questions.

A wave of nausea took hold of his stomach as he saw them pointing to a piece of paper. There was no doubt about it now. They had to be looking for him. Slowly, he turned around and started walking away. He had to warn Leila.

With each step, he expected a voice telling him to

stop; it took all his willpower to resist going faster. Only when he was safely out of sight did he allow himself to run. Leila's tent was halfway across the camp, but he found her already walking in his direction as he approached. One look at his face and she knew at once that something was wrong.

"Police," he said, panting to a stop. "You were right." His voice was shaky with panic. "I think they're looking for me."

"Are you sure?"

"Come." He took hold of her arm. "You can see for yourself."

The officers were still by the camp entrance. They seemed unwilling to come in any further as if they didn't trust the dishevelled appearance of the tents and their inhabitants. Mico had stopped at a safe distance so that they could watch without the risk of being sighted. Leila drew a sharp breath as she spotted them.

"What are we going to do?"

"I don't know," said Mico. The camp was big enough to hide in but for how long? The police wouldn't stop looking. Eventually, they'd move away from the entrance. Then what? They'd come back. They'd keep coming until they found them.

"They're only questioning the men so far," he said slowly. "Maybe they didn't get a good look at you."

At that moment, the officers started walking in their direction. Mico and Leila ducked down behind a washing line. The officers stopped.

"Who are they talking to?" said Leila, peering from behind a pair of jeans.

"The Ghost-Men," hissed Mico as she wriggled beside him. "Keep *still*. They'll see your rucksack."

182

They watched in silence as the police brought out the piece of paper. The Crow hardly even glanced at it before shaking his head. Mico was not surprised. Since their encounter by the trees the Crow had probably seen a hundred faces. It wasn't likely he would remember Mico's.

The Lizard took a little longer. Mico licked his lips. Did he know it was him? No – he was shaking his head too.

The officers spoke to them a little longer. Then the Lizard took out a wad of money and slipped it into their hands. A few seconds later, the police went back to their car and drove off.

"They paid them," said Leila. She sounded confused. "Why would they do that?"

"Guess they don't want any trouble," said Mico. In truth, the exchange had left him with a gnawing edge of unease, but he wasn't sure why. Leila stood for a moment, her lips pursed as she tried to find some reason for what they had just witnessed. Then she shrugged.

"They're gone now anyway."

Mico detected an audible tinge of relief in her voice.

"That man – suppose he can't have been that serious," she continued, talking more to herself than to him. "The police wouldn't have accepted a bribe if he was really hurt."

Mico would have liked to point out that her sense of justice, however noble, didn't always work in the real world. That sometimes there was more bad than good, more wrong than right, and there was nothing a person could do about it.

Perhaps she sensed his feelings for she turned away almost immediately.

"We should get the tools. Don't want anyone else to find them."

As they headed for the trees, Mico glanced back over his shoulder. But the Ghost-Men had already disappeared.

Their first task was to get the boat cleaned up. Along with the used paint pot, Mico had also discovered a torn shirt behind their tent. It was filthy and stank, but it made a decent rag. While Leila cleared out the leaves, he started on the scrubbing. To his surprise he found himself enjoying it. After months of waiting around a tent it felt good to finally do something with his hands.

They worked mostly in silence. It was quiet among the trees and they didn't want to run the risk of somebody overhearing them.

By the afternoon, they were hot and tired.

"I need a drink," said Leila, sitting back against the tree. Her face was flushed and sweaty. Although she hadn't said anything, Mico knew her foot was still hurting.

"I'll go," he said quickly, wiping his hands on his trousers.

"Aysha keeps a couple of bottles of water in the tent. I should have brought them with me but I forgot. Got these though."

She pulled out two crisp packets from her rucksack.

"Better be quick, monkey boy," she teased. "Or I'll finish them without you."

Leila's mood had improved significantly since that morning. Unlike Mico, she seemed to have been reassured by the exchange they had witnessed. But he wasn't so sure. What if the Lizard *had* recognised him?

He had just left the shade of the woods when he spied the Ghost-Men. He cursed inwardly. Why were they still in the camp? They weren't looking for him, surely?

At least he hadn't been spotted yet. He bent his head low, hoping to walk past them, but it didn't work. As he drew closer the Lizard glanced his way.

"Hey, you. Boy!"

Mico's heart drummed painfully as they drew nearer. The Lizard knew. He had to.

"What you doing in the trees?"

The question was like an accusation.

"I – you know." Mico tried to look embarrassed. "Had to take a leak."

The Lizard smirked and scratched his nose. He had a boil under his left nostril which danced up and down as if it was trying to escape.

"You hear about the mess we had to clean up last week," he said. "Some fool being clever. Hid himself under the tyres of a truck. Tried to hitch a lift for free. We scrape him off the ground with shovels."

Mico kept quiet. He had heard the story from Hassan already. He wondered why the Lizard was telling him. Was it supposed to be a threat?

The Crow was growing impatient.

"We got a new shipment coming in half an hour," he drawled. "Let's move."

The Lizard ignored him.

"The police were here earlier," he said, stroking a dirty fingernail against Mico's cheek. "Looking for a thief. Picture look a bit like you."

185

Mico forced himself to hold the Lizard's gaze. His palms felt sweaty.

"I haven't stolen nothing," he said.

"They say a thief broke into a house. Took some wood. A few tools."

"Wood? They gonna build something to eat? Should have taken something better. Like food. Money."

The Lizard ran a thoughtful tongue over his lips. His eyes smouldered like two black coals.

"They hurt someone too. It was in the papers." His nail pressed against Mico's skin. "Our work hard already without them sending more patrols. I run this place. Nothing happen here without my permission."

"I told you," said Mico, pulling away. "I didn't steal nothing."

The Lizard laughed unexpectedly.

"Relax," he said, patting Mico's head. "The police must be wrong. You a clever boy. You wouldn't be so stupid."

There was something about the way he was smiling that made Mico desperate to get away from him.

"I have to go," he said. "My uncle's waiting for me."

"Mhhm. Better be quick, then."

Mico could still feel the Lizard's eyes boring a hole into his back as he walked away. Did he know he was lying? Is that why he'd smiled like that? But he had no proof. The only real evidence had been the sketch and that wasn't enough. At best, he probably had a hunch.

Although it wasn't cold, Mico found himself shivering. He wondered if he should tell Leila what had happened. But what was there to say? That he thought the Lizard suspected him because he'd smiled funny? It sounded bad enough in his head.

He raised a hand to his cheek. The Lizard's nail had left a thin graze on the skin, a warning. On impulse, he swung round towards his tent. He didn't care what Leila thought. He would feel much more comfortable if he had his knife with him.

28

Over the next couple of days the boat finally began to take shape. It was slow, tiring work. Leila helped when she could, but when Aysha stayed in the tent it was left to Mico. It took him nearly a full week to cut the boards to the right size, but at last they were done.

The next morning it poured with rain. Mico stuck his head out of the tent to find the sky a soupy vat of grey. It had overturned and spilt, transforming the camp into a swamp of mud and puddles. He swore and retreated back into the tent. He'd been hoping to start nailing the boards down, but it was too wet to work today.

Inside, Hassan was inspecting his shoes. The soles had come off from the bottom a week ago. When he walked they flapped up and down like fish gasping for air. The day before he'd queued the whole morning to get a new pair. But they'd run out of his size.

Sy was counting money. He'd been at it for the last couple of days, counting, recounting, counting again. It was driving Mico mad.

"How's it look out there?" said Hassan.

"Like a swimming pool."

"Good. Then the police won't bother to come. I'm getting sick of watching them." He grimaced as he slipped his shoes onto his feet. His toes stuck clumsily out the front, the nails cracked and coated with dirt. A thin scar ran along his forehead where the doctors had stitched him up. He'd even stopped cutting his hair. Mico noticed all this with a twinge of sadness. This was not the same Hassan who'd wanted to be a film star. This one was a shadow, an empty, beaten shell.

All of a sudden Sy slammed down his fist. A fountain of notes exploded into the air.

"It's not enough. I'll never get on a truck like this. I need more."

"You could try asking for a discount," said Mico dryly.

Sy flashed him a dirty look and started stuffing the money back into his coat. He stood up abruptly.

"Where are you going?" asked Hassan.

"Omar's. I need a drink."

His departure was followed by an uneasy silence.

"He's a good man, you know," said Hassan after a short pause.

"If you say so."

"It's this place. It changes people." Almost without thinking, Hassan touched his cheek. The bites on his face had gone, but they had left faint marks that would never heal. "Look what it's done to me."

Mico shook his head.

"Sy hasn't changed. He's the same as he always was. You think he brought you from that protest because he cares? He did it because he was too scared to leave you behind. Probably thought you'd rat him to the police and get him arrested."

189

"I don't believe that."

"Then you're stupid. Sy doesn't give a damn about anyone."

"He's not the one who has a knife."

Mico blinked, taken aback. He hadn't realised Hassan knew.

"That's for protection."

"Against who? This place is too small for enemies."

Mico stared at him. It was as if he was seeing Hassan properly for the first time. He was older, but part of him was still so naïve. Had he forgotten about the Ghost-Men? The police? Or was he really dumb enough to think there were no bad guys?

For a moment, he was tempted to slap him. Give him a good shake and tell him to wake up. Then it occurred to him that perhaps Hassan knew all this already. Perhaps he *chose* not to see things as they really were. That way he could pretend the camp was how he wanted it to be. In a way, he was doing exactly what Mico did when he stepped out with his knife. Protecting himself.

They were silent for a minute. Then Mico shrugged.

"Maybe it's not as small as you think."

☆ ✿ ☆

By the afternoon the rain had stopped. Faint beams of sunlight were starting to push their way through the clouds as Mico walked through the camp. Everything was drenched. It struck him that rain in the real world wasn't like rain in stories. It didn't make stuff glitter or shine. It just brought out the dirt.

Leila was sitting outside the tent with her sketchbook balanced across her lap.

"Don't talk," she said as Mico approached. "I'm almost done."

With a decisive flourish she lifted her pencil off the page.

"There." She held up the book. "What do you think?"

Mico narrowed his eyes. All he could see were tents and a washing line.

"It's the camp."

"I know that, genius. I'm asking you what you *think*."

Mico sucked a breath of air into his cheeks as he thought of something smart to say. After a moment, he blew it out again.

"I don't know anything about art."

Leila threw him an ugly look.

"You know about the camp. Do you think it's real enough?"

"Does it matter?"

"Course it *matters*. I want to remember this place exactly as it was."

"Why?"

"Because when I'm a famous artist I'll have to give interviews about my life. I don't want to forget anything. It has to be right."

Mico almost laughed out loud.

"No-one will care about this place," he said.

"This isn't for other people," replied Leila, almost crossly. "This is for me."

She closed her sketchbook.

"Forget it. How far are we with the boat?"

Mico glanced at the tent.

"Don't worry. She's asleep."

"The boards are done," he said, keeping his voice low. "We've still got to hammer them down. Then we need to think of a way to get the boat out of the trees."

"What about food and water?"

"I'm working on it."

Leila pursed her lips together.

"Have you still got that jacket from the shed?"

"Yeah, why?"

"One of Aysha's friends needs one for her son. She brought a suitcase of food with her. She'll be happy to trade some of it, I think."

"When are you telling Aysha about the boat?"

"Soon."

Mico raised his eyebrows.

"I'm waiting for the right moment," said Leila defensively.

"We've only got a few weeks before summer's over," said Mico, sticking his arms across his chest. "We can't cross the Channel in winter. It'll be suicide. The longer you leave it—"

"I know," snapped Leila. "I'll do it when I'm ready."

Mico would have liked to point out that she had said the same thing last week but he kept quiet. They weren't going to get anywhere standing around arguing.

"I'm going to do some work on the boat," he said finally. "Meet me there when you can."

Leila said nothing as he turned to leave, but she caught up with him a few minutes later. She must have walked pretty fast because her cheeks were red and her breath all scratchy.

"I forgot to tell you. Aysha's had enough of me being in the tent. She thinks I'm a bad influence on the baby. And my foot's almost healed so there's no reason to keep me inside anymore. As long as I'm back by evening."

"Good. Then you can help me fix the hole."

He could feel Leila watching him, but he forced himself to look ahead. After a minute or two, she nudged his shoulder.

"Sorry," she said. "I'm just nervous. If Aysha says *no*…"

The word hung between them like a black cloud.

"She won't," said Mico. "Not if you talk to her. Make her see that we don't have any other choice."

"It's going to be dangerous."

"Are you having second thoughts?"

"No," said Leila emphatically. "I just—" She bit her lip, uncertain if she should air her doubts.

"Remember the man on the beach? What if we don't make it?"

Her voice dropped as she spoke so that the question came out like a whisper. Mico looked at her. Leila's hair was matted with dirt; streaks of mud were visible on her rucksack which was no longer bright yellow, but a sort of sad murky bronze. He remembered the first time he had seen her. Then, she had sparked like a star, strong and bright, but now she seemed so tired. Like a fire that no longer had the strength to burn. If they didn't leave soon, he worried she might extinguish altogether.

Lightly, he touched her arm.

"We have to try," he said.

29

By the weekend the hole was nearly finished. Leila waited as Mico positioned a nail into place then she held the two halves of the oar into the air.

"How are we going to fix this?"

"We don't," said Mico.

He lifted the hammer.

"We've still got a board left. I'm going to try cutting one out of that."

"Only one?"

"There's not enough wood for another—" He stopped, ears pricked.

"Do you hear that?"

"Hear what?"

Mico put a finger to his lips and motioned Leila to listen. Her eyes widened as she heard them too. In the distance – somewhere to the left of them – voices. They were drawing closer.

"It's not fair."

Mico stiffened in recognition. It was Sy.

"I got us a bottle last time." His words slurred on top of each other. "It's your turn."

"I got no money," whined a second, drunker voice.

"You never get anything do you, Omar? *Sha*, like a leech you are. Sucking me dry. I've seen that watch you keep under your pillow. Why don't you trade that, eh?"

Mico bit his lip. Neither of these men were in their senses and that made them dangerous. Almost without thinking, he tightened his grip on the hammer. Whatever happened there was no way he was going to let them take the boat.

Sy and Omar seemed to have stopped. He could hear them on the other side of the trees arguing with each other. Then a low thump. Mico felt something twist in his gut as he heard it a second time. As if someone was bashing their head against a tree. Then a shout. Running footsteps.

Suddenly, Omar burst through the trees in front of them. Mico hardly recognised him. The top of his head was coated with blood. His eyes were red and wild.

"Get back here, Omar!" yelled Sy. He uttered something in a foreign language.

Omar's face was twisted in panic. All at once, his eyes fell on Mico and Leila. Mico stood up and flexed the hammer at him in warning. Omar blinked stupidly.

"I'm leaving," shouted Sy again. "If you want to spend the night out here you can."

With a sudden jerk of the head, Omar gave a frightened little yelp and ran off. Mico stiffened in anticipation, certain Sy would now come for them. But Omar was even less sober than he'd thought. A barrage of swearing exploded into the air as he ran past Sy – then more footsteps.

Silence returned to the trees.

"I think they've gone," whispered Leila.

Mico took a deep breath and sat down. Thin ridges had formed on his palm from where he'd been holding the hammer. Leila gave a strained sort of laugh.

"That was close."

Mico was still looking at his hands. The hammer sat on the ground in front of him. He felt sick.

"You wouldn't really have used it," said Leila. But she didn't sound too sure.

"I wasn't going to let them take the boat," said Mico quietly. "We've worked too hard on it."

"Lucky he was so drunk." Leila didn't quite meet his eye. "He must have thought he was dreaming."

"Yeah," echoed Mico. "He must have."

Although neither of them mentioned it, Omar's appearance weighed heavily on their minds. Mico could tell by the way Leila kept throwing glances over her shoulder that she was still worried about him. Every so often, Mico would also stop and listen, half expecting to hear footsteps drawing towards them. It wasn't just Omar that concerned him. The longer they kept the boat in the trees the bigger the risk of anyone discovering it.

Over the next few days, they worked harder and faster than ever before. It was as if they were racing an invisible beast. If they didn't get the boat ready soon the beast would catch hold of it and swallow it whole.

But they could not outrun it forever. A week later, the beast caught up with them.

Mico was trying to cut an oar out of the remaining wood. It was proving harder than he'd anticipated, mainly because the handsaw he'd taken from the shed was too unwieldy for such a delicate job. Leila was using a rag to daub paint onto the outside of the boat.

"How far do you think it is?" she asked.

Mico did not need to ask her what she meant.

"Far enough," he grunted.

"Yes, but exactly?"

Before Mico could reply, the handsaw got stuck. He swore and tried to pull it along the wood. Almost at once, the blade snapped.

"Damn."

With some difficulty, he wrenched it free from the wood but it was obvious the blade was beyond repair.

"Now what?" said Leila.

"I'll have to use my knife."

He began reaching for his pocket before he realised he'd left it in the tent.

"I'll come too," said Leila as he stood up. "This paint's giving me a headache."

They dragged some foliage across the boat then set off through the trees. They had only gone a few steps before Mico felt a strange tingling sensation on the back of his neck. He whipped round, expecting to see Omar, but there was nobody. The trees looked back at him, empty and unseeing, like rows of hunched witches.

"What's the matter?"

Leila was watching him curiously.

"Nothing," said Mico. He touched his neck. "I thought someone was behind us."

Leila smiled.

"You said you don't believe in ghosts."

"That's right," he replied, pushing thoughts of Esther's tree-spirits out of his mind. "I don't."

They hurried back through the camp. Mico was

annoyed at himself for forgetting the knife. Now that they were so close to finishing the boat they couldn't afford to waste time. Every minute counted.

"If we get everything ready by this evening we can tell Aysha," said Leila as they entered the tent.

Just then, Hassan appeared in front of them. He looked terrible. Wild strands of hair hung across his face and his cheeks were smudged with tears. Leila drew back in alarm as he seized Mico's shoulders. Words tumbled out of him in an incoherent babble.

"Slow down, Hassan," said Mico. "What's happened?"

"Sy's gone."

Mico was so surprised that for a moment he didn't know what to say.

"Maybe he should sit down," suggested Leila.

Together the two of them helped Hassan to the floor.

"What's wrong with him?" Leila whispered. "Do you think he's ill?"

"I can't believe he's left," muttered Hassan, though it was difficult to tell who he was speaking to. "He'd been talking about it for months but I never really thought he'd go through with it. Everyone knows how dangerous the trucks are."

"I thought he didn't have enough money," said Mico.

Hassan shook his head.

"He didn't. But I met Omar just now. He told me Sy had made a deal with the Ghost-Men."

A cold blade twisted in Mico's heart.

"What deal?" said Leila.

"I don't know. He just said that Sy kept bragging about how he was finally going to be able to leave. I thought he looked happy. Ever since he got back from his walk yesterday—"

"Walk?" interrupted Mico sharply. "What walk?"

"Why does that matter?"

"Where did he go, Hassan?"

"I don't – I can't remember."

Mico grabbed hold of Hassan's shoulders and shook him roughly.

"You have to," he said. "It's important."

"Mico…" began Leila.

"Where did he go?"

"I told you," cried Hassan. "I don't know. Towards the trees, maybe."

Mico didn't wait to hear anymore. He ran. Far behind, he heard Leila calling his name, but he didn't stop. All he knew was that he had to get to the boat.

30

He was too late.

As he reached the spot where the boat was hidden he saw two figures already bending over it. One was holding the hammer.

Mico gave a strangled cry and sprinted towards them.

"Don't touch it," he shouted.

The figure with the hammer was the first to turn around. Mico stopped in his tracks. In the silhouette of the trees the Lizard's face glinted silver like stone. His eyes flashed in recognition before settling into a cold, black stare. Seeing him in the hollow filled Mico with a sickness so great he found himself shaking.

"Get away from our boat," he snarled.

The Lizard smiled and passed the hammer to the Crow. Mico's heart dropped as he came forwards. The boat was in pieces. All the hard work they had put into it lay scattered across the ground like dead leaves. It would never float again.

"I warn you, boy," said the Lizard. "You should have listened."

Mico was so angry he could hardly breathe. A howl grew and died in his throat as the Crow smashed the last remaining boards. The noise of the hammer splintered through the air. Each strike was like a little stab in his heart. He shut his eyes, reminded of another scene, another moment of destruction.

Far away he heard footsteps approaching then a low shriek.

"No," moaned Leila, stepping past Mico. "No, no, no…"

The Lizard stood to one side, a thin smirk playing on his lips. Leila turned towards him. Tears glittered in her eyes.

"Why?" she asked. "Why would you do this?"

The Lizard gestured to Mico.

"I told him. Nobody get in or out this camp without us." He kicked the boards. "You think you're clever, eh? You think we won't find out?"

Leila flushed.

"My sister's having a baby," she said quietly.

"Babies cost extra," drawled the Crow.

The Lizard stepped forward and jabbed her in the shoulder.

"Understand one thing, girl. We are the only ones who get you across the water alive. If you want to leave, you pay for it. Nothing comes free in this world."

"It wasn't yours," said Mico. The Lizard didn't appear to hear him.

"When your friend come and tell me about a boat in the trees, I thought he was crazy. But he said he

201

show me if I help him leave. We got him on a truck this morning. Smart, he was. Not like you."

Mico clenched his fists. But Leila beat him to it. With an enraged scream she threw herself onto the Lizard. Surprised, he stumbled and fell, raising his hands as she aimed a punch at his face. The Crow stood up, hammer in hand. Mico reached for his knife.

Before either of them could move, the Lizard lashed out with his leg. Leila flew backwards, tripped and hit the ground. A sharp crack, like a gunshot, rang into the air as her head smacked against a rock.

"Leila?"

Mico scrambled towards her, his heart beating like a drum. A thin line of blood trickled down her cheek. He shook her gently, but her eyes remained closed.

"Stupid girl," hissed the Lizard, rising to his feet. "You never make it in this thing—"

He was cut off as Mico's knife clamped across his throat.

"Don't you speak about her like that," he said fiercely. "Don't you dare."

The Lizard made a strange gargling noise and flapped his arms against Mico's chest. The Crow came forward, wielding the hammer, but Mico was ready for him. He kicked out and heard a cry of pain as his foot met something soft. Out of the corner of his eye he saw the Crow drop to the floor.

The Lizard clawed at his wrists. Mico hardly noticed. A bubble of long-held rage had erupted inside him. He could feel it running through his veins, hot like lava, lending him a strength he didn't even know he possessed. He pressed harder. He had nothing more left to lose.

202

The knife leered hungrily against his opponent's throat. All it would take was one flick—

"No, Mico!"

Hassan was already out of breath as he thundered to a stop. Mico ignored him. He wasn't going to leave the Lizard, not today, not after what he'd done.

"We need to help Leila."

Mico took a deep breath, willing the blade down. The Lizard gasped and grabbed at his hands.

"Don't," said Hassan softly.

A line of blood was just starting to blossom under the steel. Mico stared at it, then looked up at the Lizard's eyes. For one sickening moment he saw his own reflection staring back at him. With a cry of defeat, he pushed the Lizard away.

Hassan was already trying to get Leila to her feet.

"She's unconscious," he said. "We'll have to carry her."

Mico nodded, his eyes fixed on the blood hardening beneath Leila's head. There was a faint rustling behind him as the Lizard vanished into the trees. The Crow moaned quietly.

"What about—?" began Hassan.

Mico shook his head. He took one last look at the knife and dropped it in the grass. Then he slid his arms underneath Leila's shoulders.

"Let's go."

They stumbled through the trees in silence. Shadows loomed at them from either side, picking at their faces like bony fingers. Mico could hear Hassan panting behind him, but he pressed on, faster and faster. Leila had already lost a lot of blood. They didn't have time to waste.

Outside the clinic there was the usual line of people

waiting to be seen. Mico barged straight past them into the tent.

"Help," he shouted. "My friend's hurt."

Within seconds a nurse was in front of him.

"I'm sorry. We don't have any more beds—" she started to say, then stopped as she caught sight of Leila. At once her manner changed.

"Lie her down here," she ordered, pushing aside a couple of chairs and putting a clean sheet down in their place. She disappeared as Mico and Hassan lowered Leila to the floor, but returned immediately with another older lady.

"I'm Dr Morris," said the woman, bending down. Her fingers moved swiftly across Leila's head. "You want to tell me what happened to her?"

"She—" Mico hesitated, unsure where to begin. Should he mention the boat? The Ghost-Men?

Dr Morris seemed to read his mind.

"I don't care about the details," she said. "But I need to know how she got this injury."

Mico shrugged helplessly.

"She fell. Hit her head on a rock."

"What's her name?"

"Leila."

"All right. Leila?" The doctor shone a light into her eyes. "Can you hear me? My name's Dr Morris. Leila?"

There was no reply.

"She's going to be OK, isn't she?" said Mico.

Dr Morris didn't reply. A frown had appeared on her face, pinching her expression into an inscrutable mask. She barked some instructions to the nurse who scurried away.

"We should tell her sister," said Hassan.

"I'm not going anywhere."

Hassan nodded as if he'd already known what Mico was going to say.

"I'll be back soon." He touched him lightly on the shoulder. "Leila's a fighter. She'll get through this."

Mico tried to believe him.

It didn't work.

"I forgot her rucksack," he said dully. "She's going to be mad at me when she wakes up."

The nurse was back almost as soon as Hassan had left. She wasn't alone. In fact, it seemed as if she'd brought all the clinic staff with her. Mico found himself pushed back against the flow of people as instructions thundered through the air. He watched as they stuck needles into Leila's skin. A bag of transparent fluid was strung up beside her. In the middle of it all Dr Morris was still throwing out questions.

"Leila? Can you hear me? Leila?"

"Maybe I can try," said Mico, but the words were lost at the back of his throat. Dr Morris hurled more instructions at her staff – *zip zip zip* – like a gun firing bullets. Mico tried to speak, but people in white coats kept blocking his view of Leila. The staff were in a frenzy, a wild rush of anxious faces, open mouths, rubber gloves.

Mico didn't wait to see what happened. He ran. So fast that he didn't even see Aysha and Hassan – didn't hear them shouting his name.

Past the tents, out the entrance – further and further until pavements and streets blurred beneath his feet – until each breath was like a knife in his chest.

He should never have listened to Leila. If they hadn't tried to fix the boat – if he hadn't found the damn thing to start with – if Sy hadn't betrayed them.

205

Finally he had to stop. Bent over, panting like a dog.

It took him a few minutes to realise where he was. Opposite him the police station was illuminated by a few windows of light. Mico glared at the building in disgust. Police. Lawyers. Governments. They were supposed to protect people. But when had they ever helped him?

At that moment a couple of officers walked out of the building. Their laughter rang out in the air, loud and careless. Just like that, something in Mico cracked. Someone had to pay for what had happened to Leila. Someone had to take responsibility. Why shouldn't it be them?

Instinctively he reached for the knife but he had dropped it in the trees. Instead, his hand closed on a few pathetic stones. He bit his lip, thinking back to the afternoon when Leila had given them to him. He'd slipped them in his pocket and forgotten all about them. He looked back at the officers. They were heading towards a car parked some distance away.

"This one's for you, Leila," he murmured under his breath. He started to run.

His arm shot into the air, swung back and snapped forwards.

"Eat rock, y'kalb!" he roared.

One stone got the officer's shoulder. The next couple smashed through the car windscreen.

The officers dived for cover.

Mico charged.

He could almost feel Leila running beside him, egging him on. *Go on, monkey boy*, she whispered, grinning sideways at him.

Mico crashed into the first officer like an arrow,

straight and true, sending them both tumbling across the ground.

"She's dying," spat Mico.

He shook the officer's shoulders.

"You're the police. You're supposed to help people."

The man rattled out a long string of French words and tried to push him off, but Mico held on fast.

"Listen to me. You've got to do something! She's my friend!"

With the admission came the tears.

"You have to get us out of here. Please."

He was sobbing now, his shoulders heaving up and down as he thought of Leila back in the clinic. Was she going to die? Was he about to lose her like he'd lost everyone else? First Esther. Then Razi, the Doctor—

Suddenly he felt someone pulling him backwards. He was only vaguely aware of the circle of people standing around him. They barked at him in French then one kicked off in English. Mico hardly heard them. The world felt like it was spinning. Sick and exhausted, he turned his head up to the sky. The arms around his shoulders were wings; if he closed his eyes, they could take him anywhere. All the way to the stars.

Eventually the officers hauled him into the station. Papers were shuffled – signed – stamped. One took him into a room and asked him questions he didn't know how to answer. Mico stared at the table as the words chimed around him.

"We can put you away for a very long time," threatened the officer in English.

Mico said nothing. He no longer cared.

31

The door to the cell opened with a loud clang. Mico stirred. For a second he felt as if he was still on the boat, the Lizard strolling on the deck, banging a rod against the floor to keep them quiet. He opened his eyes. The cell sneered back at him, an unwelcome reminder of the truth.

An officer stepped inside.

"Get up," he said, not unkindly. "You've got a visitor."

Mico's hands were cuffed. In silence he was led into another room, empty except for a table and two chairs. The officer sat him down then stood back against the wall, arms folded across his chest. Minutes later, the door opened. Mico looked up as Aysha entered the room. She appeared older, impossibly so, as if they were meeting after years not days. She sat down and studied him for a long moment, her eyes sweeping over his face. It was obvious she'd been crying.

The realisation filled him with shame. He'd tried so hard to do what Uncle Abu had told him. To find a new life for himself. To be strong. Like Esther. But he'd failed. And Leila had paid the price.

"You shouldn't have attacked those officers," said Aysha at last.

Mico looked down at his hands. He felt sick.

"They wanted to charge you with assault but I explained what happened at the camp. There is no excuse for what you did but in light of the circumstances the police have agreed to grant you bail. You'll be released tomorrow. We'll have to come back to clear all this up but at least you won't have to stay here."

Mico licked his lips. Why was she being so kind to him? Was it because of Leila? He squeezed his eyes shut as he remembered the last time he'd seen her. Lying on the floor, blood stuck to her head. His breath caught painfully in his throat. Is that why Aysha was here? To judge his guilt? Is that what this was?

Aysha sighed.

"Look at me, Mico."

He shook his head.

"Please?"

It took all of Mico's willpower to move his eyes up to her face. He blinked. She was smiling.

"You want to see Leila, don't you?"

Mico opened his mouth to reply but the words fell away from his lips.

"She's OK, Mico."

"I don't understand. The doctor—"

"—moved her to the hospital in time. They're confident she's going to make a full recovery."

"I thought—"

Tears stung at Mico's eyes.

"It was my fault she got hurt. The boat – I never meant – but Sy…"

Aysha took hold of his hands and hushed him gently.

"Hassan told me what happened. You're not to blame. In fact, I should thank you. If you hadn't got her to the clinic so quickly anything could have happened."

Mico could hardly speak. Since that night he had been falling, drowning in an unspeakable darkness, but now a great weight had lifted off his shoulders. He felt strangely light, as if he was floating on air.

"Whose idea was it? To fix the boat?"

Mico thought of the bird they'd carved into the wood.

"Ours," he said simply.

"Did you really think it would work?"

Mico was surprised to find he had no answer. During the time they'd spent fixing the boat he'd been convinced that it was their way out. But now he wasn't so sure. What had it all been for, he wondered, if not to escape? Had it just been a distraction? Something to divert their attention from life in the camp? But no – he had sat in the boat that day. He had tasted the salt on his lips, felt the waves beneath him. He had allowed its song to soak into his bones. How could he explain to Aysha? That feeling?

"Leila told me a story once," he said. "About the first humans. She said they were born with wings."

Aysha looked taken aback. Mico wondered if she was thinking about Jahir, if she was cross at Leila for sharing this piece of his memory. But when she spoke it was with a tone of pride.

"That girl," she murmured. "Once she gets an idea in her head, she won't let it go. I should have kept a closer eye on her."

"None of this is your fault." The last thing Mico wanted was for Aysha to blame herself. "It's not anyone's fault. Sy's, maybe."

Aysha looked unconvinced.

"I only hope this one won't give me so much trouble," she said, laying a hand on her stomach.

"She'll have Leila to watch out for her," said Mico.

"Yes," said Aysha, her lips twitching at the certainty in his voice. "Yes, she will. Thanks to you."

"Is it true you want to stay in France?"

"I am thinking about it."

"Is that what you want?"

"What I want?" echoed Aysha. Her eyes tightened as she spoke. "I have wanted much, Mico. To change the past, to put everything back to what it was. But some things are not so easy to fix. Sometimes, it doesn't matter how badly you want. It's never enough."

"That's not fair," said Mico. Then, as if it could solve everything that had happened, "It's not right."

"No," said Aysha. "It isn't."

She smiled unexpectedly.

"You might be happy to know that Sy didn't make it very far. A police patrol stopped his truck on the motorway and dropped him back."

For some reason, Mico could find no delight in this news. He had lived with Sy for so long, but listening to Aysha speak of him was like hearing about a stranger.

"What about Hassan?"

"They let him out of the clinic yesterday."

At Mico's look of puzzlement, she shrugged.

"Him and Sy had a big fight. Sy's moved in with Omar now."

Her voice shook with menace.

211

"If he's got any sense, he won't dare come in front of me."

Mico did not know how to reply. It struck him that people never quite did what you expected. It didn't matter where they were from. They would always surprise you.

"Hassan asked me to tell you he's got a new pair of shoes," continued Aysha. "And he wants to start a little theatre for the kids. Teach them a bit of acting, singing. Madness! It's food the children need."

"Maybe it's not for the kids," said Mico slowly. "Maybe he's doing it for himself." He paused. "What about the Ghost-Men?"

"Nobody's seen them for days."

"They'll be back," said Mico, remembering how he'd almost killed the Lizard.

"Maybe," said Aysha. Her eyes glinted with steely defiance. For a moment, Mico thought he saw Leila sitting opposite him. Then she was gone.

"Last night, a boat was stopped by Greek police. It was in the newspapers. Two smugglers were arrested. The report said they were coming this way. No pictures, though, so we can't know for certain."

Mico absorbed this information in silence. Could it be true? Then it occurred to him that it didn't matter.

"Even if they've got them, there'll be others," he murmured. "As long as there's people desperate enough there'll be Ghost-Men waiting, ready to snap them up."

Beside them, the officer coughed and motioned to his watch. Mico hesitated, remembering the fate of the boat. But he had to ask.

"What happens now?"

212

Aysha regarded him steadily.

"I don't know," she said. "Your case will take time. A couple of weeks, maybe. There may also be a court hearing." She squeezed his hands. "I wish I could tell you that everything will be fine but I cannot. You understand that, don't you?"

Mico was quiet for a second. In his mind he watched two figures rise up off the ground, their wings trailing a glorious blaze across the sky. Above the horizon they turned and waved. Then they vanished.

For the first time in what felt like forever, he smiled.

"Tell Leila I'll see her tomorrow."

ACKNOWLEDGEMENTS

I am extremely grateful to the following people: Laura Stimson, Michelle Spring and the wonderful people at Writers' Centre Norwich who started me on my way; Nicola Upson, fellow thinker and tea-drinker, for sharing her wisdom and laughter; Jo Hayes, for believing; Lauren Gardner, agent-cum-ninja, who pushed the boat out in every way; Megan Duff, for helping build the manuscript into so much more. Also, for her patience.

A big thanks also to Afshan, Jasmine, Priyanka and Henna, who probably thought I was crazy but never said it.

Finally, I owe a huge debt of gratitude to my family for reading all my stories, even those I never finish. Thank you for showing me how to fly.

For anyone looking for a way to help, The Bike Project is a wonderful charity which donates bikes to refugees and asylum seekers. Find them @The_BikeProject or thebikeproject.co.uk